THE BEAUTY OF THE DESERT, FROM A LAWMAN'S PERSPECTIVE, IS THAT THERE AREN'T A DOZEN HIGHWAYS CRISS-CROSSING. CLOSE FOUR ROADS, YOU LIMIT THEM TO A HUNDRED-MILE RADIUS.

The web gets smaller ...

Twenty miles outside of Gallup, a dead bicyclist on the highway. One blast from a moving car. Neon-bright Spandex made him a great target. Still, it was pretty good shooting. He'd been down less than an hour – I drew my net tighter. A ring circling the city, with me at the center.

No doubt about it. Mickey Knox, you'll meet Jack Scagnetti tonight, you bastard.

Natural Born Killers

A NOVEL BY
**John August and
Jane Hamsher**

BASED ON A STORY BY
Quentin Tarantino

AND A SCREENPLAY BY
**David Veloz &
Richard Rutowski &
Oliver Stone**

WITH AN INTRODUCTION BY
Oliver Stone

Ⓢ

A SIGNET BOOK

SIGNET
Published by the Penguin Group
Penguin Books USA Inc., 375 Hudson Street,
New York, New York 10014, U.S.A.
Penguin Books Ltd, 27 Wrights Lane,
London W8 5TZ, England
Penguin Books Australia Ltd, Ringwood,
Victoria, Australia
Penguin Books Canada Ltd, 10 Alcorn Avenue,
Toronto, Ontario, Canada M4V 3B2
Penguin Books (N.Z.) Ltd, 182-190 Wairau Road,
Auckland 10, New Zealand

Penguin Books Ltd, Registered Offices:
Harmondsworth, Middlesex, England

First published by Signet, an imprint of Dutton Signet,
a division of Penguin Books USA Inc.

First Printing, August, 1994
10 9 8 7 6 5 4 3

PUBLISHER'S NOTE
This is a work of fiction. Names, characters, places, and incidents either are
the product of the author's imagination or are used fictitiously, and any
resemblance to actual persons, living or dead, events, or locales is entirely co-
incidental.

Author's Note

Where possible, situations and dialogue have been reconstructed through recordings or interviews with participants, witnesses, and survivors. In other cases, a degree of fictionalization has been used to connect missing story points. The author suspects these moments will be readily apparent to the reader in context.

While there are countless people to thank, special notice must be given to Hardt/Empire Books for permission to reprint a portion of Jack Scagnetti's unfinished novel; and to the family of Katherine Ginniss, who generously allowed us access to her personal files. Without their cooperation, a major facet of this story could never have been told.

NATURAL BORN KILLERS

Introduction
Oliver Stone

When we set out to make *Natural Born Killers* in late 1992, it was surreal. By the time it was finished in 1994, it had become real. In that warped season of the witch, we saw Bobbit, Menendez, Tonya, O.J., Buttafucco, and several dozen other perverted celebrities grasp our national attention span. Each week America was deluged by the media with a new pseudo-tragic soap opera, insuring ratings, money, and above all continuity of the hysteria.

When Tonya Harding finally made the front page of the newspaper of record, the *New York Times,* some *five* or *six* times for what was essentially an act of minor vandalism, we must've all subconsciously sensed that the Age of Absurdity would close out the American Century. "The ancients had visions," Octavio Paz recently wrote, "we have television. But the civilization of the spectacle is cruel. The spectators have no memory; because of that they also lack remorse and true conscience . . . they quickly forget and scarcely blink at the scenes of death and destruction of the Persian Gulf War or at the curves of Madonna or Michael Jackson. . . . They await the Great Yawn, anonymous and universal, which is the Apocalypse and Final Judgment of the society of spectacle. . . . We are condemned to this new vision of hell; those who appear on the screen and those of us who watch. Is there an escape? I don't know. One must seek it.''

Tomorrow—tonight—Mickey and Mallory Knox can happen, without doubt. And they too would have their hour in the sun—and by the next two issues of *TV Guide* would give way to the next predator in the ratings war, which like the presidential polls that monitor the president's daily bowel movements, become sort of the equivalent of the ''popularity contests'' we all had to suffer through as kids in grade school. The deserts, as I remember, never went to the deserving but to the gossiped-about, which is more important to the American psyche than to be perceived as an A student. The banker, as we learn in our culture, is unknown and unpopular; Billy the Kid is not. Only the Greeks created great victims in their dramaturgy—Elektra, Medea, Antigone, and Oedipus we are not. But we *are* a race which *inflicts,* we are people who *do* unto others—Vietnam, sports, lawsuits, come immediately to mind. Violence is salvational in the American epic tradition, at least it was in Fennimore Cooper and Jack London and Hemingway. The law of survival, the natural law, now perverted by the PG-money business mining the gold hills of ''family entertainment'' movies with sanitized violence and safely preaching to us that violence is incorrect. Is it? Or it is just the way of the world—the world where under every peaceful blade of grass, tiny yet feral bugs devour other bugs in orgiastic cycles of destruction and creation?

Eddy Vedder wrote: "In the days of old suicide was enough . . . just to end their own suffering. Now there's a need to see another suffer . . . as innocent as they once were . . . as helpless as they are now. We have created a monster . . . a herd of monsters."

No legislation in Washington, no TV or movie censor boards are going to prevent these merging virtual realities of media from expanding. It is inevitable that with games, viewing glasses, interactive buttonry, more and more "news" and what's-happening-every-nanosecond-shows, that the depiction of violence will become more and more realistic. As television and some movies banalize their violence (no squibs, no blood, no shock to the act of dying), the news shows will win the ratings war with carpet coverage of murder. As there once was C-Span and the Court Channel, an Execution Channel is inevitable for gassings, lethal injections, "night before" and "last meal" dramatics. Crimes will be exactly reproduced with new film science.

(Note, of course, Robin Andersen's [of Fordham University Communications Department] observation that while TV's "reality cops enjoy a success rate of 62 percent, FBI statistics indicate only 18 percent of crimes are actually resolved. The plots, which most often feature the restoration of justice through force, send a clear message: Aggressive behavior by cops toward suspects is necessary to protect law-abiding citizens from dangerous minorities . . . we are empowered by it. When the police force their shouting into a house, throwing the occupants down on the floor and tackling "suspects," we feel the surge of excitement at the moment of confrontation. We are on the side of state-sanctioned power.")

But we did not set out to do this in *Natural Born Killers*—to depict the violence naturalistically. I have done that in *Platoon, Born on the Fourth of July,* and *JFK*. And I have seen the crime formula expertly drawn in films like *In Cold Blood, Henry: Portrait of a Serial Killer, Reservoir Dogs,* and many others. I accept the overwhelming evidence of the reality of crime around us (though statistics show that violent crime has actually remained flat; Department of Justice Statistics, which I believe more accurate than FBI figures reveal violent crimes per 1,000 people at 32.6% in 1973 and 32.1% in 1994). But in accepting the post in *Clockwork Orange*/Sam Peckinpaugh zeitgeist of dramatic crime, what I set out to do was satirize (i.e., reflect through exaggerating, distorting with dark humor for effect) the painful idea that crime has gotten so crazy, so far out of hand, so numbing and so desensitizing, that in this movie's Beavis and Butthead 1990s America crimescape, the subject approaches the comedic, as does the media which so avariciously covers it.

Our society is bloated not just with crime but with media coverage of it. But bloated also with the madness of selling more and more armaments to the world, the madness of massive buildup of prisons to house the "criminal subclass," an anti-crime fervor that creates unusual sentencing such as "three strikes and you're out," drug laws that are particularly hypocritical and idiosyncratic state to state. Cops, wardens, prisons, reporters—they all must sense they have become part of a vast and bizarre web of cruel, totalitarian punishment. In this environment, it is inevitable that lone killers like Mickey and Mallory, anti-heroes to the core, will rise to the surface of a

facelessly oppressive system and capture the
hearts and minds of Americans looking for a
human face—be it Bobbit, Buttafucco, or Anita
Hill complaining about the injustice of modern
life. Kafka was wrong—the individual is no
longer crushed or faceless as long as he can get
on TV—game show or murder, what's the real
difference? When you're in jail all your life, a
moment in the sun is a moment in the sun.

Mickey and Mallory are, yes, irreverent and
unguilty, drawn broadly in a Swiftian/Voltairian
caricature of our worst nightmare. But they do
"come" from violence. Violence is depicted as
generationally handed down from father/mother
to son/daughter and on and on. To the end of
time. There will be no end to violence. But something particularly vicious about the twentieth century stands out in its faceless, genocidal quality
and in trying to show those seeds of Hitler and
Stalin and Vietnam and Armenia, etc., we have
planted the idea in the numerous rear-projection
images of the film, that we are all swamped in this
century, looking as Paz said earlier, to "get out."

I did not seek to dwell in or glorify their violence, although I will be accused of such. I believe the cuts are fast, the film nervous as it
should be; nothing is meant to upset the stomach
as perhaps our *Scarface* chain-saw scene or *Mid-
night Express* tongue-biting scene did; no, I think
the shock is ideological—the idea that a situation
like this can exist repels certain people, from
either side of the political spectrum. But satire, if
it's working, *should* be about shock.

Always an alternate or subversive idea upsets
the mind of the time. Didn't Kubrick and *Clockwork Orange* offend the perceived borders of
violence? Did not, years before, Buñuel and Dali

with a mere eyeball and razor shock and offend? Eisenstein with a baby carriage and a shattered eyeglass? It is, I think, a question of style. All subjects under the sun go round and round. The Greeks got there first—and with buckets of blood and gouged-out eyeballs. I don't think we should artistically differentiate between subject matters. An eyeball and a razor are as important as state control of aggression in *Clockwork Orange*. A man dying of AIDS, the Russian Revolution, or a "natural born killer" let loose on the world by an insane system and media, it is all behavior sanctioned under the same sun that has ruled our minds since the first gas and dust violently collided. Once we outlaw subjects as "politically correct," we begin—and have begun—the process of undermining our basic freedoms.

Yet I do believe there is love at the end. And I do believe that, in one of our characters' words, "love beats the demon." Without giving away our ending, I find it ironic that it is Mickey and Mallory who are the ones to escape the Great Yawn. But you make up your own mind.

"In a dark time, the eye begins to see."
—Theodore Roethke

CHAPTER

1

Rumbling like an angry god, a red 1970 Dodge Challenger 383 Magnum RT, with black bumblebee pinstriping, eased into a prime spot right by the door of the Kankakee Sonic.

It was the kind of thumping engine drone that makes a mother call her children in from playing on the lawn.

The sound of a storm gathering on the horizon.

A sound that suddenly died as Mickey Knox killed the engine.

The senior guys and sophomore girls who regularly hooked up at the Sonic, before retiring to the darkness and privacy of the reservoir, stopped to gape in awe at the sight of the two newcomers. For certainly, these two weren't from around here.

Eighteen-year-old Mallory Wilson climbed out of the car without saying a word, ignoring the stares of every man, woman, and cheerleader at the Sonic that Friday night as she walked toward the restaurant. Between her halter top and hip-hugging jeans lay thirteen inches of bare white skin, so taut and smooth it looked to be carved from a single piece of ivory. And in the center of this beauty lay her navel, an indentation that every hormone-choked male adolescent in the parking lot that night would have loved to press, if only to see what recoiled in his face.

There was no doubt about it: The girl reeked of sex and danger.

When Mallory stepped inside, that left only Mickey Knox to stare at who, with his tinted John Lennon glasses and ripped jeans, looked like a young Timothy Leary on steroids. He carried himself with the cocky swagger of a dime-store hood who'd watched one too many Lee Marvin movies. The kind of guy who was born guilty. And couldn't care less.

These were the coolest people who had come to Kankakee, ever.

The normal chatter of the twenty or so teenagers outside Sonic that night was quieted for the duration of Mickey's brief but potent walk to the front door. Until suddenly, quite unexpectedly, freshman Randall Krevnitz spoke:

"That is the coolest car I've ever seen."

Mickey Knox kept walking. To everyone's fear and surprise, Randall spoke again, louder this time.

"Is that your car, man?"

Mickey Knox stopped dead in his tracks. Removed his glasses. "Are you asking if I stole that car? Is that your question?'' He spoke with the slow cadence of a trailer-park mafioso, punctuating each syllable even as he slurred them together. ''Then, no. Paid good money for that car there.''

''It's beautiful, man. Three thirty-five horsepower?''

''No, it ain't quite stock,'' said Mickey, who seemed to enjoy the subject of his car. ''It's got a low-end, Mopar, purple three-quarter race cam, a set of hooker headers, and a Mallory dual-point ignition. Did the work myself. Had it dyno-tuned, and they rate it at about 390 now.''

''I'd kill for a car like that.''

''Would you, now?''

''Hell, yes.''

Mickey Knox smiled. He was even more intimidating when he smiled. ''Come to think of it, so would I.''

Police later reconstructed the cash register receipts to determine that Mickey Knox had ordered two cheeseburgers, a hamburger, a Coke, and a Diet Coke, totalling $5.86. He broke a fifty.

Bud ''Tiny'' Wilkins, the manager on duty that night, kept a television tucked under the counter so he could watch his favorite shows, while Jimmy in back fried up the orders. Seven years ago, when he first started bringing in his mother's out-of-focus TV, the owner wouldn't let him watch during peak business hours. After a few months, however, the owner relented, because television was really the only thing the poor man had in his life. Bud "Tiny" Wilkins was not a short man, which led to natural speculation as to how he earned his nickname. That he never married only fueled these rumors.

Mickey Knox stood silent as his order was being cooked, watching a rack of shiny greased hot dogs rolling endlessly under a heat lamp.

Had Tiny Wilkins been watching Action 7 news that night, he would have seen a live report from correspondent Ally Bree, the harsh camera lights washing out the dry wrinkles around her eyes as she described the scene behind her: three police cars, a crime scene investigation unit, and the coroner's wagon in the distance. Uniformed police officers were stringing a second band of yellow tape round the two-story house on 113 Hickamore Lane, a line running from the bent post of an old picket fence to a dead oak with the letters "M & M" carved into it.

Had Tiny Wilkins been watching News 9 that night, he would have heard Ruth Mambers, next-door neighbor to the deceased, explain why that evening in particular she had decided to confront Ed Wilson and his wife about their daughter, Mallory, her ex-con boyfriend, and the Marlboro cigarette butts she kept finding on her lawn every morning. When no one answered the doorbell at the Wilson house, she had taken it upon herself to look in the kitchen window, discovering the bloodshed inside.

Had Tiny Wilkins been watching NewsStar 4,

he would have seen a full-screen photo of Mickey Knox taken from the Lansing High School yearbook as the reporter described how Ed Wilson was forcibly drowned in a ten-gallon fish tank. He would have learned that police in five states were looking for Mickey Knox and Mallory Wilson. He would have known that his life was in immediate danger.

Tiny Wilkins was watching Fox.

"Couldn't you just fuck Kelly Bundy?" he asked Mickey as he handed him back his change. "I mean, look at the way she hikes up her ass like that. So fucking hot. And you just know old Al's getting some of that. A little nibble here and there."

Mickey filled a Styrofoam cup half full of ketchup from the stainless-steel pump at the condiment bar. He shook a layer of salt on top of the ketchup, then kept pumping.

Tiny continued his thought. "Think about it—how come Al never wants to fuck his wife? You know why? Because he's doing his daughter. It's true, I swear to God. And you know why you never see Kelly's room on the show? Because it's S & M central, that's why. Whips, chains, everything. He takes her back there, ties her up, and gets off. Think about it. You're Al Bundy, your life is shit, you got nothing to live for. Why not taste a little of your own doing? It's his daughter, it's his jizz that made her in the first place."

"Sort of like sucking your own dick," said Mickey.

"Abso-fucking-lutely. I'd be the happiest man in Illinois if I could do that."

"You can," said Mickey Knox as he swirled the salt into the ketchup with a straw. "Trust me, you can."

The women's restroom at the Kankakee Sonic was stocked with an arsenal of haircare products unseen by most Americans in the post-Nancy Sinatra era. Chief among these weapons was the forty-eight-ounce canister of Aqua Net, $2.39 at Wal-Mart, which reigned queen over all other big-hair options. Providing not just volume but wind resistance, crucial for convertibles and pickup truck beds, Aqua Net offered a wispy hardness that no mousse or gel could rival.

With such power, however, came responsibility, which is why the women of the Kankakee Sonic had designated the front section of the restroom by the sinks and mirrors a "no smoking" zone. As Kankakee legend had it, a freshman several years ago had her hair burned down to the roots when a slipstream of Aqua Net had ignited on a nearby cigarette. The girl's hair never grew back, and she was forced to become a lesbian in Missouri. While the story was probably apocryphal, there was in fact an enduring social contract among the Sonic women: smoke in the back, *before* spraying your hair.

Which is why when Mallory lit her Marlboro

by the sinks, she broke a social taboo on a par with murder and giving head to a freshman. As the only senior in the restroom, it was up to Tina Hopkins to enforce the law.

"Put that fucking thing out," she told Mallory, not a trace of trepidation in her voice. The other girls unconsciously took a step back, clearing space should nails be drawn.

"Excuse me?" asked Mallory. "What did you say?"

Tina didn't repeat herself. Instead, she reached forward calmly, plucked the Marlboro from Mallory's lips, and drowned it in the stream of water gurgling in the sink. The cigarette butt with the orange-red lipstick marks swirled in the drain for a moment before being sucked under.

The restroom was silent. Tina and Mallory locked eyes for a long moment, two snakes circling each other in the sand. Tina was holding her own against the new girl, the out-of-towner with her too-thin waist and fuck-me boots. Her stature among the women of the Sonic would surely rise after the incident, as the legend spread how Tina Hopkins had stood down the bitch who had come to steal their boyfriends.

Mallory broke the gaze first, pushing past Tina for the stalls. A clear win for the Sonic side. Confident in her victory, Tina spoke the words "fucking cunt" as Mallory locked the door to the stall.

As she peed, Mallory could hear the murmurs and chittering whispers around her, all talking about her. Judging her. Comparing her. There was a squelched laugh that provoked giggles and "shushes." Still peeing, Mallory took her orange-red lipstick and drew an "M & M" on the back of the stall door, surrounding the letters with a big thin heart.

The toilet had flushed completely before she flipped open the latch to face her enemies, arranged like a gauntlet between her and the door. She walked up to Tina, paused right by the exit, and said with a sweetness in her voice, "Can I ask you something?"

Tina didn't say anything, just smiled a little.

"Are you sorry for what you just did?"

With her back arched and her hair at full height, Tina was a good two inches taller than Mallory. "You are a fucking little whore," she said.

Mallory backed off a step. A certain sadness came into her eyes as her hands curled into fists. "See, I hate that. I really hate it when people fuck with me. You know why? Because a girl just can't go through life getting fucked without fucking back."

In a single motion that could only be instinct, Mallory grabbed Tina by roots of her sticky hair, pulling her off balance, and simultaneously landing a fist just below the sternum. The wind knocked out of her, Tina was in no shape to fight back when Mallory began slamming her head against the air dryer. Cracking the mirror in two places, Tina's head next came crashing against the edge of the porcelain sinks. Coroners later estimated that her death came by the fourth blow, out of a total of eleven against the sink, wall, and floor. A wrist was also broken, although it's not known how.

Freshman Kerry Jacobsen was closest to the door. While the rest of the girls watched, stunned, she managed to get the door partway open before Mallory sent her slamming back against the trash. Two ribs were cracked by the force of the door.

"And just where do you think you're going!" shouted Mallory, her accent noticeably more white-trashy the louder it got. Pinned between the door and the wall, Kerry was helpless to fight as Mallory yelled out into the hall: "Mickey! Baby, come here!"

Hearing Mallory yell to him, Mickey dropped the two Cokes and the cup of ketchup, kicking the latter accidentally as he ran. It left a thick red streak across the white tile floor, a smear that would later be mistaken for blood by the newly hired deputy coroner.

By the time Mickey reached the restroom door, Mallory was in the process of grinding the heel of what was to become her trademark, a platform suede thrift-store boot, into the cheek of Tina's lifeless face, a triumphant brand that left no question as to exactly who the victor had been in this particular altercation. The rest of the occupants were huddled against the back wall like puppies in a thunderstorm. Two cheerleaders locked themselves in a stall.

With his .357 drawn, Mickey looked over to Mallory in surprise. "Where's your .22?" he asked.

"I forgot it in the car," said Mallory.

"You *what?*"

"Okay, okay, so I fucked up," she said. "I was only going for a pee."

"Mal," said Mickey, in a somewhat patronizing tone, "if I'm gonna have to. . . ."

"All right, all right, already!" said Mallory. "Are you gonna take care of this or am I gonna have to go back out to the car while you stand around and yap?"

Mickey released the safety on the .357.

"Just tell me who, baby."

Mallory frowned a bit; her voice had a squeal of wicked joy to it. "All of 'em."

Stunned like deer caught in the headlights, the co-captains of the drill team fell first, followed by the valedictorian. Kerry Jacobsen made a surprise charge at Mickey that caught him off-guard; Mallory had to pull her off his back, kicking her twice to get her to hunch up in the corner, where she was an easy shot. To keep busy, Mallory sprayed Aqua Net at two girls who cringed like it was acid. Their suffering didn't last long.

Bathroom stalls were designed for privacy, not protection, so one kick sent the door flying open. The two cheerleaders inside, Mary Proctor and Judy Kane, were both standing on top of the toilet, shaking. Mickey pulled the trigger, one shot penetrating both women, who slumped against opposite sides of the stall.

Judy Kane, the blonder of the two, was lucky; Mary's body had stopped the full force of the bullet from ravaging Judy's entrails. Surgeons at nearby Kankakee General Hospital were able to reconstruct her during sixteen hours of surgery.

She was the only survivor of what came to be known as the "Kankakee Bathroom Massacre."

As Mickey and Mallory made their way out of the bathroom and to the exit, Jimmy, the cook, had the initiative to think of grabbing the fire extinguisher as a possible weapon. Unfortunately he had never attended the mandatory Sonic fire safety lecture, during which he would have learned to pull the red pin before squeezing the handle. With the pin in place, the handle didn't budge, which gave Mickey the opportunity to land a slug directly in the canister. The resulting explosion left two inches of bloody foam in the hallway by the pay phones.

But "Tiny" Wilkins put up no fight whatsoever. Two quick cuts with a hunting knife left him bleeding uncontrollably. Mickey may have toyed with the idea of making good on his earlier threat, but probably had neither the time nor the interest to unzip Tiny's Lee jeans. Instead, he took one of the hot dogs rolling on the rack and fed it to him, letting him pretend.

Out in the parking lot, where the sound of gunfire had not been heard over competing broad-

casts of "Mony Mony," all-country quarterback
Troy Hallowell was leaning on the Dodge Challenger, looking at the tapes scattered on the seat.
Gun drawn, Mickey made him step back from the
car before shooting him. The seats were only
vinyl, but still.

Pulling the .22 from the glove box, Mallory
hunted the west side of the Sonic lot with deadly
accuracy, while Mickey took the east. Everyone
ran, but it's hard to outrun a bullet.

Tailback Larry Dean fumbled his chance at survival.

"Hey you," Mickey said to the fear-stricken
boy. "There's two kinds of people in this world,
Ford and Chevy. Which one are you?"

"I . . . I dunno," blubbered Larry. "Ford?"

"Wrong answer," said Mickey. He snapped
the barrel shut. "Now if you'da said Chevy, I
might have let you live."

In the end, only Dodge enthusiast Randall
Krevnitz survived the assault on the Sonic parking lot, writing an award-winning eulogy for the
Kankakee High yearbook.

The rest of his friends were dead.

CHAPTER

2

Detective Jack Scagnetti arrived at the scene at 3:25 A.M., escorted by a phalanx of screaming police cruisers that blazed the trail for him the last hundred miles from Chicago, testament to the potential, untapped speed of the American highway system. With the pavement nearly empty at this hour, other law enforcement officers might not have found the need for screeching sirens, but to Scagnetti, the piercing two-tone whine was one of God's most beautiful sounds. It pumped him up with a rush of euphoria that no chemical could duplicate, though God knows Scagnetti had tried. From a mile away, it announced to the world that trouble was coming. Fear, awe, and death. At Judgment Day, the angels of the apocalypse wouldn't be riding horses, but driving behind the wheels of Ford four-door sedans.

Scagnetti's contingent joined the swarm of police cars, ambulances, and coroners' wagons surrounding the Kankakee Sonic. A fire truck was also stationed close by; a grease fire had erupted in the untended kitchen, a situation that could have been handled easily but for the lack of a fire extinguisher.

Three heavily caffeinated Explorer Scouts were working the road, keeping the growing crowd of reporters off the parking lot. Recognizing Scagnetti, they rushed to clear an opening for him to pull in, pushing back a crew from CNN as they were starting a live feed.

A scrub-faced deputy named Jimmy Hale met Scagnetti at his car, walking at his heels as they cut through the spiderweb of police tape that stretched from every available post and corner.

"Detective Scagnetti, I just want you to know that you're probably the reason I became a cop," said Hale. "I read your Scarwin book and I guess it changed my life. I mean, I *know* it changed my life."

Scagnetti had to wait at the doors to the restaurant as two tagged bodies were being wheeled out.

"What you said about having to think like a killer, I try to do that every day. Sometimes I'll just be somewhere, and I'll sit there, and I'll think, 'What would I do right now if I was a psychopathic killer?' Or, 'What would Jack Scagnetti do?' " Hale had hoped for a smile, a reaction, something out of Scagnetti, but the detective wasn't paying much attention to him.

"I was reading this book by Anthony Robbins,

and he was saying the way to success was to find someone who could do something really well, and model yourself after them. And I guess I'd like to think I'm modeling myself after you."

Scagnetti lit a cigarette with a match. Only thirty-five years old, graying at the temples, and gut spreading in ever-expanding waves around his midsection, he had the voice of a man who had been smoking since he was ten (which was true).

"What about *Scagnetti on Scagnetti*?"

"Oh, yeah. Liked that book a lot. A whole lot. I sure did. I was really surprised when it didn't sell better."

Hale later recounted that Scagnetti had then handed him the still-burning match. He cradled the flame with his palm like it was a sacred gift.

"It was the greatest moment of my life," said Hale. "I don't care what anybody said about him later. That was the act of a great man."

Scagnetti slapped him on the back and smiled. "Coffee, black," he said. "And make sure there's no blood in it."

Although Scagnetti had no official jurisdiction in Illinois, there was no question he was the point man for the Mickey and Mallory murders. No less than the governor himself had called, tracking Scagnetti down through his literary agent finding him in a seedy strip joint on the south side. Two hundred miles of speed, sirens, and a few grams of DEA-confiscated "evidence" had sobered him up to the point where his hangdog stare could be mistaken for intense concentration.

At the time the governor found him, Scagnetti was no longer on the government payroll, but was being supported by the American public, which had eagerly dropped $24.95 for the first hardcover printing of his true-crime epics. Although critics had panned his latest work, *Scagnetti on Scagnetti,* for being little more than a self-promoting rehash of the F. Scarwin case, it still shipped 750,000 units its first week. His appearance on *Montel Williams* drew the highest ratings for the sweeps week, bolstered perhaps by the staged confrontation between him and three women who claimed to be simultaneously pregnant with the artificially inseminated children of Richard Ramirez.

With ample amounts of blood, sex, and rock-'n'roll, the Mickey and Mallory murders were just what it would take to put Scagnetti back on top. His publisher was already lining up ghost-writers to work on the book. (*Scagnetti on Scagnetti* was the first and last book Jack would ever write solo.)

Scagnetti had followed the route Mickey and Mallory had taken just hours before as they blasted their way through the Kankakee Sonic, starting with the women's restroom. Coroners had already begun to bag and tag, but masking tape outlines and bloodstains offered a pretty good picture of how the bodies fell. For instance, Mickey had killed the two cheerleaders with one shot, and that was pretty funny, Scagnetti thought to himself. You had to admire that kind of style.

By his own account, he was the first cop there to think of checking inside the stalls. Mallory had obviously headed to the restroom for some reason, after all. On the back of the second stall door, he found the lipstick heart Mallory had drawn: M & M. *Bet she's sweet as candy,* Jack thought. *Melts in your mouth.*

He caught his reflection in the cracked mirror as he passed, the spiderweb fractures surrounding a crater where all the threads came together. He couldn't tell for sure whether the lines he was seeing were leading *from* the impact or *to* it. But there was a trace of blood in the center. He caught himself looking at this pattern, looking at himself. And laughed.

Jack Scagnetti's fascination with murder came not by choice, but by a strange twist of fate.

Seven days after his fifth birthday, young Jack Scagnetti was walking across the campus of the University of Texas, on the way to the library where his mother, a student teacher in the Austin public school system, had checkout privileges.

It was shortly after noon, and unbeknownst to Jack or his mother, architectural-engineering student Charles Whitman had just arrived at the observation deck of the tallest building in Austin, the very University of Texas watchtower where Jack and his mother were now headed. Whitman carried with him a footlocker containing a 6mm rifle with a telescopic sight, a Remmington 35-caliber pump rifle, a .357 magnum pistol, a 9-mm Luger pistol, a 30.06 reconditioned army carbine, a 12-gauge, sawed-off shotgun, and a large Bowie knife.

Once atop the tower, Whitman—for reasons that were never known, other than the fact that he was carrying a heavy academic load of four-teen units that semester and it seemed to be weighing heavily on his shoulders—began picking off people on the ground below him with deadly accuracy.

One of the first to die was Katherine Culip Scagnetti. There was not even a sound as her chest exploded and she hit the ground in front of little Jack, the shots originating twenty-seven stories away. A brave stranger grabbed Jack and threw him into the bushes before running for cover himself.

In his second book, *Scagnetti on Scagnetti,* he told the story of lying in the bushes all day, covered with ants while he gazed on his mother's dead body. In fact, it took only an hour and fifteen minutes until the police stormed the obser-vation deck and killed Whitman, but few wanted to take the lawman to task for exaggeration in the wake of the overwhelming tragedy that sur-rounded it.

Vengeance became his obsession; as a police officer given to twisting the rules to serve his own ends, his violent past was frequently invoked to excuse his behavior. The public embraced him as a symbol of intolerance to the ever-expanding culture of violence that gripped the country as the twentieth century came to a close. His fellow officers thought of him as something of an embarrassment—a hot dog whose disregard for procedure was barely compensated for by his almost innate ability to get under the skin of a killer and think like him.

It seemed like a gift.

But maybe not.

With no surviving witnesses to describe what happened inside the restaurant, Scagnetti was left with only Randall Krevnitz to piece the story together. Dumbshit psychiatrists could hold Randall's hand for the next five years while he wondered why he couldn't keep an erection and how come the world had to be so damned awful, but right now Scagnetti needed answers.

He wrapped an arm around the boy's shoulder and took him out of the commotion. Scagnetti stood a few inches too close to him, violating his personal space, so the kid couldn't just zone out on him. He offered Randall a cigarette, which he took, but the boy didn't make any move toward putting it in his mouth. He had never smoked.

In an almost holy trance that Scagnetti had seen just once before (in himself) Randall described how Mickey and Mallory Knox had arrived that night: the thunder, the exhaust, the rumble of horses restrained within the Chal-

lenger. *I'd kill to have a car like that*—he had
said exactly those words to Mickey Knox. And
the thing was, he would have killed Mickey if
he'd had the chance. Not out of hatred, or fear,
or self-defense, but because he wanted that car.
By killing him, becoming him.

Scagnetti asked about the girl. Was she a hostage? Was Mickey forcing her to do this, or was
it her own free will?

"I'm sure she was forced to do what she did,"
said Randall after a long pause. "They made her
do it."

"Mickey, you're saying. Mickey made her do
this shit."

Randall's eyes went wider as he looked down
and to the side, replaying the night like a loop in
his mind. "No, I mean *them*. The people inside.
Whatever they did, you know they did something
they shouldn't have. I mean, who's to say who's
right and all, but I couldn't say for certain that
Mickey and . . ."

"Mallory."

Randall smiled a little, hearing her name.
"Couldn't say for absolute certain that what they
did was wrong. Kind of unfortunate, I guess. I
mean, probably everybody didn't deserve to
die." Snot was running out of the kid's nose,
which he wiped off with his sleeve. "But when
you think about it, probably a lot of them did, so
who's to say?"

Scagnetti leaned in close. The kid could probably still smell the whiskey on him. "Can you

tell me why, out of all these people, they let you live?"

For the first time, Randall looked him right in the eye.

"Guess I didn't deserve to die."

With an eerie tranquility, he held up the cigarette he'd been fingering for a light. His hands weren't shaking at all. Drawing in the flame from Scagnetti's match, Randall Krevnitz didn't choke one bit.

Pulling away from the Sonic that morning at 6:35 A.M., Jack Scagnetti headed for the Motel 6 nine miles east of Kankakee. He had to fight his natural instinct just to keep driving, looking for his killers (west, they had to be going west, why do outlaws always head west?) when police in five states were looking for them, two very obvious killers in a very obvious car. Logic dictated they would be caught by sundown.

Yet they couldn't be. Logic didn't hold in this instance. People like Mickey Knox have the power to bend the rules of nature and coincidence around them, making a fool out of the inevitable. Scagnetti knew they would slip through the net, roaring past while a cop reached for his coffee. Like him, they were born to die. But die brilliantly.

They would still be there when he woke up.

The hunt was just beginning.

CHAPTER 3

Wayne Gale was a happy man.

Happy, happy, happy.

Truth be told, he had never been particularly unhappy at any given moment of his life. He was born into a loving and nurturing middle-class family in Melbourne, Australia, who encouraged Wayne to capitalize on his wit and charisma. He had moved to America and married a lovely and supportive wife, who, despite being unbearable, had given him entrée to his chosen profession. In many ways, his life was proceeding quite well before this last bit of news.

Yet Mickey and Mallory were his salvation. An answer to his prayers. If he had believed in God, he would have kissed Him full on the lips just for taking the time to make such truly perfect beings. Fresh. Deadly. Telegenic. And uncaptured.

Wayne Gale was the host of *American Maniacs*.

The show had been on the air only two months

the night the Wilson parents met the hereafter (it was, in fact, playing on the television set when police first entered the house), but already the lurid tabloid had seen its ratings plummet to one tenth of its premiere. Granted, its premiere was a one-on-one interview with Charles Manson, but the longevity of the show at the network was called into serious question. Neither Wayne nor the producers would admit it, but the show's very concept was limited. There was only a short list of A-list psychos to choose from, and not a lot news happened to them behind bars.

Adding to the downward spiral came a blistering article in *Entertainment Weekly,* which singled out *American Maniacs* and Wayne Gale in particular as embodying everything that was wrong with television today. Wayne didn't take it too personally, except for the jab about his fake Australian accent. It was very much real. It took a lot of work here in America to keep it from decomposing into mid-Atlantic dreariness.

Latest gossip among the eleventh-floor secretaries (two of whom had a thing for Wayne, being cute in a scrappy, stray dog sort of way) had the network boys sliding the show into a 9:30 P.M. slot after the new Bronson Pinchot vehicle, a midseason replacement. It was certain death.

Until Mickey and Mallory came along.

When he got the call, Wayne was hanging upside-down from the ceiling of his Manhattan apartment, ignoring the advice of his structural integrator, Inge, who had warned him repeatedly not to return to his old habits of gravity boots before bedtime. He did so in the false hope that it would make him taller, really the only physical trait that caused Wayne to be less than happy, happy, happy. "Your spine vill loose its alignment," Inge had cautioned. To Wayne's peers, it was news that he even had a spine.

The call came at 12:20 A.M. from Wayne's producer, Julie, whom he immediately switched over to the TTY machine. Wayne wasn't deaf. Julie was born without a tongue.

Together with Roger on camera and Scotty with sound, the *American Maniacs* team flew out of La Guardia at 1:47 A.M., headed for the Kankakee Sonic and a date with destiny. And ratings.

Wayne Gale was a happy man.

Even in situations like this, Julie was careful to book Wayne's seat away from the other three. Despite having worn out two frequent flyer cards, Wayne still got giddy on planes, a documented physiological change that made him the Most Annoying Man on Earth. Actually, any enclosed space had the tendency to bring out this phenomenon, but something about the roar of the engines and the air pressure on his eardrums made plane travel with Wayne particularly unbearable.

Wayne Gale had three things he talked about on planes:

1) his childhood.
2) his ambitions, and

3) his show, *American Maniacs,* 10 P.M., Wednesdays.

Eileen Murchovsky, a construction accountant from Arlington Heights, was treated to an hour and a half of the first topic on her red-eye home. She vowed never to fly again.

A dwarfish, wiry child, Wayne Montclaire Galenovitch won a starring role in *Wally the Wallabee,* a short-lived spinoff of the Australian television hit *Skippy the Bush Kangaroo.* The show went off the air after only ten episodes, but it was enough to make Wayne a minor star and begin his infatuation with being in front of the camera.

Through his teenage years, Wayne "Gale"—as he shortened his name to the dismay of his parents—went on to play small parts in minor sitcoms and dramatic series, usually playing the geeky love interest to the teenage daughter. Often he was written out of the show with a fatal, incurable disease after just a few episodes. His demands for sharper dialogue and better camera angles didn't sit well with the producers.

During his later teens, Wayne returned to common society on the outskirts of Melbourne. Too small and clumsy to hold his own at the local high school, he frequently found himself the target of various bullies' aggression, who extorted lunch money and term papers out of him. It was only as the editor of the high school's newspaper, the *Queen's Cross Tattler,* that Wayne found release.

His six-part expose on school lunches resulted in the firing of the entire kitchen staff, while photos documenting the homosexual affair between headmaster Colin Waverly and French teacher Jacques-Pierre Dumas resulted in classes being cancelled for two weeks while the entire faculty was investigated by local police and church officials.

At eighteen, Wayne turned down an offer to become a field production assistant at the venerable *Australia Weekly* (a cross between *60 Minutes* and *The McLaughlin Group*) to get in front of the cameras as a correspondent for *Public Eye,* a trashy upstart financed by a Singapore conglomerate. By contract, every third episode had to feature someone being killed or maimed by a competitor's faulty product. Wayne spent two sixty-hour weeks trying to find anyone in Australia injured by a non-Holofil pillow. His "Down of Death" segment was probably the apotheosis of his early career.

When *Public Eye* folded, he packed his bags for America, playing second string for two ill-conceived syndicated tabloids before landing as anchor of *American Maniacs.* Actually, he was the network's second choice, but the top contender was forced out of television by reports that he was living conjugally with a high-profile, married—actor. Had he done his homework on Wayne more carefully, the fallen anchor might have suspected the source of the leak.

While the show was still in development, differ-

ent set colors being tested against Wayne's ever-
changing tan, he met and fell in love with Delores
Morgan, who, quite coincidentally, was the network president's daughter. After a brief, torrid
affair, they eloped to Mexico one week before
the show premiered. Returning to the States,
Wayne found himself with a hit television show,
bags of fan mail, and a wife who was frighteningly
ordinary. Not just boring, but boorish.

But that was a different conversation. As the
plane touched down in Chicago, Wayne asked
seatmate Eileen Murchovsky what she did for
a living.

The crew arrived at the Kankakee Sonic at 6:15
A.M., fighting for parking lot space with local
station and several network affiliates. With a loud
aerosol boat horn, Wayne interrupted three separate live feeds, including his own network's A.M.
show. Yet his tactic was successful, clearing a
way for his crew all the way up to the yellow
police lines, where he could begin arguing with
the police to be let inside.

Surveying the scene and tallying the body
count, Julie made a quick cellular conference
call, locking down a special half-hour time slot
for that night. They had never done a same-day
shoot, but by commandeering the affiliate truck,
she was sure they could get the show ready for a
partly live 10:30 slot.

Seeing Scagnetti about to leave the scene,
Wayne yelled to him across the parking lot, trying

to get him to come over for an interview. Jack squinted his eyes against the bright morning sun to see who was calling his name. Realizing it was Wayne Gale, he gave him the finger, shouting ''Fuck you, Wayne!'' at the top of his voice. For Jack Scagnetti's fateful encounter with Wayne Gale over the Mickey and Mallory Knox Case was not his first. The two had a history.

A few years earlier on Wayne's first American show (*Supercops!*), his profile on Scagnetti brought up allegations of police brutality, sexual misconduct, and misuse of evidence. All this from what the show's producers had described to Scagnetti's publicist as a glowing puff piece. The report probably cost him $50,000 in legal fees in a storm of personal injury suits and fueled critics' attacks on *Scagnetti on Scagnetti*. To Wayne, it was water under the bridge. To Scagnetti, it was still Niagara Falls.

That night's special edition of *American Maniacs* drew a thirty share, easily crushing the competition, which included dueling Victoria Principal movies of the week (*Too Young the Child,* in which she played the mother of a terminally ill boy, and *Beyond Belief: The Constantine Euvornos Story,* which told the true story of a surrogate mother fighting for custody of her terminally ill girl). Scagnetti was left out of the report except for a brief image of him flipping Wayne the bird, his middle finger pixilated to keep the network boys happy. Watching the show from their motel room in Sterling, Colorado, Mickey and Mallory were surprised and impressed with their handiwork, having forgotten exactly whom they killed when. Mallory had estimated fourteen dead; Wayne put out the number at twenty.

As Mickey would report later to a cellmate at the Illinois State correctional systems' clearinghouse at Joliet, their favorite part of the whole show was watching Dodge enthusiast Randall Krevnitz recount his version of the killings, describing Mickey and Mallory as "gods of death and destruction." Almost as good was Grace Mulberry, the sole survivor of the slumber party attack—choked with emotion beyond expression.

Mallory wondered why they didn't talk about the attendant they had killed at the Boulder, Colorado, Arco station, one James Harding. Mickey had shot him in the knee before sticking the hose down his throat, pumping his stomach full of gasoline before forcing the young man to immolate himself by lighting his own Bic.

It was then that the idea occurred to Mickey that would elevate them from the crowded ranks of modern mass murderers into the pantheon of living legends.

"We'd killed everyone, that's why," recalled Mickey to his cellmate. "From then on we decided to leave one person alive to tell everybody who did this. 'You tell them Mickey and Mallory did this,' we'd say. Don't know why we hadn't thought of it sooner."

* * *

Owen Traft was the last, great untargeted de-
mographic of balding forty-year-old men who
never married. Renting his one-bedroom apartment in East Palo Alto, a tiny strip on the good
side of the freeway, he made the hour-and-a-half
commute into and out of San Francisco five days
a week, leaving at six-thirty in the morning and
arriving home at seven each night. He had done
so for the past eight years, when the industrial
supplies company he worked for announced it
was moving into the city proper. The commute
would have cut into the social plans of any other
Bay resident, but Owen had no social life.

Instead of a life, Owen Traft had a forty-five-
inch, wide-screen television with picture-in-pic-
ture and theatrical sound, custom installed by a
contractor who had to use a crane to get it
through his third-story patio door. Owen kept the
volume at a steady eight notches, the threshold
above which neighbors would start banging on
the walls to complain. He tuned into a solid
seventy hours of network, cable, and pay-per-
view each week. A two-deck VCR hooked to
the second cable line helped him keep track of
daytime TV. He had recently written to a man
featured on *Beyond 2000* who was developing a
dial-in VCR you could program by remote from
the telephone, a level of completeness Owen
sorely lacked.

If anyone had bothered to ask him, he could
have listed how many episodes of *Full House*

were now in syndication, or the name of the actor who played Stephanie Zimbalist's partner in the first season of *Remmington Steele,* plus his later credits. To him, it wasn't trivia, but simply the means to understand his kingdom inside the box. From the safety of his remote control, he ruled it like a benevolent dictator.

Yet of all the shows he had watched, this episode of *American Maniacs* was the most compelling. No, not "compelling" in the way that *60 Minutes* was compelling. Owen would have described this show as inspiring. Mickey and Mallory were like people he had always known, but never met. Charles Manson, Ted Bundy, Jeffrey Dahmer—folks who got more news airtime and inspired more made-for-TV movies than AIDS and the collapse of communism combined.

Folks who knew what they wanted out of life. Folks who, unlike Laverne and Shirley, actually *did* make their dreams come true. Owen was too slight to make the football squad in high school, too dim to be noticed by teachers, and his broad, flat head and alien eyebrows precluded him from ever having a date. There *was* glory to be found in this world, thought Owen, and right then and there he made a pact with himself to go out and get him some.

CHAPTER 4

TO: DETECTIVE JACK SCAGNETTI
        CHIEF INVESTIGATOR, SPECIAL TASK FORCE
        ON MICKEY KNOX AND MALLORY WILSON

FROM: SPECIAL AGENT KATHERINE GINNISS
        FBI BEHAVIORAL SCIENCE UNIT
        QUANTICO, VIRGINIA

I am in receipt of your memo dated April 24, in
response to my request for information regarding the
dispensation of the investigation of the Mickey Knox/
Mallory Wilson murders. While "fuck off and die, you
pencil-pushing bitch" qualifies as one of the all-time
great snappy rejoinders, I feel that such a sentiment is
ultimately counterproductive to accomplishing the
task that, for better or worse, we jointly share at
this moment.

You may be interested to know, Detective, that I
have read your books, and am familiar with your
operating style—namely, that of a maverick lone wolf

with a badge who stalks his prey on instinct and apprehends them in a blaze of testosterone-fueled bravado. This may very well be an extremely desirable quality in the leader of a high-profile special task force; it also has limitations if it effectively excludes any sort of scientific analysis of the situation that could provide valuable information.

I propose, Detective Scagnetti, that rather than be at each other's throats on this one, we work together. As you may or may not know, the Behavioral Science Unit is a team of highly dedicated investigators who are adept at drawing psychological profiles based on background interviews, site investigations, medical records, and such other information as we can glean on the suspects which can be used to predict their next moves and respond in a preemptive way, rather than a reactive method which will ultimately leave us ten steps behind the killers and the bodies they leave in their wake.

Attached for your information are copies of the interviews our field investigators have done to date. Most of the people in Mickey Knox's native Wilmington, Kentucky, were reluctant to speak about him, as he seems to come from a very tight-knit hillbilly clan who are by their very nature suspicious of outsiders and protective of their own, even when their own is a serial killer.

During the summer of 1987, however, Mickey kept company with one Donna Wooley, who seems to have been his only girlfriend before he met Mallory. Perhaps the most interesting (and revealing) chronicle we have of his personality and his latent propensity for violence comes from Donna's reluctantly surrendered diary from the period, which follows. The document dates from the summer of 1987. Her diary entries regarding Mickey contain most interesting letters which he sent to her; they are also the only written record we have where Mickey Knox speaks for himself.

If I can be of any further assistance, I hope you will please feel free to contact me.

FBI File #32061-A17   Doc. #17042
Case #914-376

1. Entries from the diary of Donna Wooley:

June 11. Dear Diary. Whew! School is finally out. With the extra week we had to make up for the hurricane, I thought I was going to be a freshman forever. Cassie and Carla and me have gotten totally "shitfaced" already three times since the last day of school, and many more good times are "on the horizon". Summer!!!. . . . There's this guy, Mickey Knox, that hangs around the the Presby Pool all the time. He never swims, he just hangs out in his cowboy boots. He tried to talk to us today, but Cassie told him she didn't waste her time with rednecks and crackers. He didn't say anything. He just spit into the pool. What a "dumbass".

June 28. Dear Diary. Time "flies" when you're having fun. I got a job at Woolworth's. It's weird working with your mom, but it's fun taking "breaks" together. After work, a bunch of us usually drive up to Spoon

Lake in Bobby's dad's "monster" truck and drink Tanquery and wine, which is my favorite. Mickey Knox was up there last night, working on his car which wouldn't start. He had a bottle of "slow" gin, which tastes like "mountain lion piss" to me, but we sat in his car and talked almost the whole night. He's definitely "different", but they say that's the spice of life. He said he would write me a letter because he hates telephones.

PS we kissed. He was okay, but he said I tasted salty.

July 1. Dear Diary. Got Mickey's letter. Finally. Here it is.

Donna. This is the letter I talked about that night at Spoon Lake when you said I was crazy as a loon. Remember? It turns out you were right, because it takes being crazy to write to someone you just met. I've been watching you at Presby Pool all the time, but since we talked, I know you're not one of the PDs (prairie dogs). They spend all their time underground, which most people do too. It makes me sick. I'm gonna live where I can see the sky and the sun and not run for my hole. Even if it's a shit sun and a shit sky.

Most people don't want to know me, and even you probably think I'm somebody who works on cars and hangs out at the pool. But I just do that to hear different voices. I hear them all the time. When I'm alone, they're so loud it's like I'm at The Trail. (You ever been there? They have a band on Tuesday nights that can fry your face off and make you beg for more, I swear to goddamn.)

Where was I? Donna, you got a lot to learn. Did you know:

1. Most people live longer than they're supposed to. They should die when their teeth fall out. That's Nature's barometer.

2. The average person lies 90% of the time. I don't, by the way. And if you ever do, you'll never see me again.

3. Apples way back when were no bigger than a cherry. Personally, I think people are too fucking hungry.

4. The earth is alive. If you poke it, it hurts. That's what earthquakes and hurricanes are. Most PDs are too scared to see this.

5. I could go on and on.

If you do good in school and listen to your parents and do everything the PDs want, you don't have anytime to figure out what you're good at. Which is where I'm at. Nobody can tell you except you, so what are you going to do?

Have you ever spent an hour completely alone? PDs are too scared, but I'm not. Are you? You might learn something awful, but that's okay too.

"A junkyard of bad ideas." That's me if you listen to the PDs.

You're salty because you're crying inside. You live like that, you won't live long. Cry it out, and you'll taste like sugar. That sounds pretty good, right? I like that idea.

Now you know the real me. My favorite show used to be MASH and now it's whatever's on. I can make tacos out of almost any kind of meat you give me, and you'll never know what hit you. I get in trouble, and I get out too. I work in a meat house, but I'm going into the Marines next year. I'm right-handed, which you'd expect.

I got to go. You can tell I'm on the level. Be prepared. Regards, Mickey Knox.''

I'm too tired to talk about this. Goodnight, Diary.

July 2. Dear Diary. I showed Mickey's letter to Bobby. He thinks it's sick and I should run not walk to the nearest exit sign. But if there are any PDs like Mickey says, it's Bobby. He kisses every ass in town, including his own, and I'd pay a dollar to see that in the circus.

Carla is pregnant. God, she's a "fucken" idiot. It's probably Gary, but maybe Bobby, she says. That's a big surprise. He never got to first base with me.

July 5. Dear Diary. I have a real "hangover". Last night was the 4th, and it was a total "party": about two hundred people went up to the old missile base and it was fun.

Before I go any further, I have to tell a secret. Me and Mickey did the dirty deed. It was a total surprise, believe me, but I liked it. He has so much energy. It's like if you touch his body, you get shocked. I must have been the fool, because every time he kissed me, I was making all sorts of noises. I think I "came"—I sure felt drained if that's what it is like. Mickey said I am not so salty any more. He has beautiful skin. We did it in the grass down a slope so no one could see, and it felt like we were "going at it" for an hour. Some "fucken" PDs set off M80s and scared me, so Mickey didn't get to finish, but he said it's okay, he'll go for double next time. I think he was scared too, but he pretended to laugh.

My head hurts too much. I'll write tomorrow.

July 18. Dear Diary. With Mickey all the time. Yesterday we drove into Fayetteville, and Mickey bought tarrow cards. He can tell our future. Day before, we "fucked" in my parents' bed and called each other my parents' names. Beth and Paul. It was creepy, but Mickey said it was a right of passage, and he was right. I don't feel young anymore.

August 1. Dear Diary. The last three weeks have been the best in my life. I have found the one person who can make me happy with just a smile or a touch of his electric body. Mickey Knox. Mickey Knox. Mickey Knox. Donna Knox? Mickey and Donna Knox? I want that more than anything.

But lately so much shit has "gone down", I want to die. Actually, one good thing happened. Mickey taught me how to poach an egg in a little red wine, and it's so good, it's all I eat now.

But Bobby. What a GD PD. He told my parents I was "dating" Mickey. Can you believe that? He drove over to my house when I wasn't there and just told them. My father thinks he's a good person, but I know he's a "fucken" prick, and next time I see him, I'm going to kick his ass real bad.

My father shit a cow. I've never seen him so mad.

He said Mickey Knox has a reputation in our town, which I never heard anything about so how did he know? He was just blabbing to sound like he knows jack shit.

My mother has a magazine article in her folder box for every occassion. Especially girls getting "laid" by older guys, it turns out. She loves me, but I'm already 15. If I don't know better by now, it's a little "fucken" late!

My father wouldn't let me out of the house for three days. Mickey threw a note up to my room the second night. He's a poet.

Donna. Part of me is dying and waiting to be put in the ground since you are locked up by your grab-ass, faggot, PD, motherscrewing father. I am now officially starting my list, and he's got the top spot. So far it goes like this:
  1. Paul
  2. My fifth grade teacher.
  3. Jamie Farr
  4. Bobby
  5. Rod Stewart
Bobby might move up. I'm not sure. I went to his house three times to kick his ass, but he's hiding out. It's a matter of time.

But don't worry, honey bunch. I'll wait for you. Hurry, though, because I don't have forever."

I had to promise my parents I would never see Mickey again, and they finally let me out. Meanwhile, Carla had an abortion and didn't even tell me. She said it was definitely Bobby's baby, but how does she know? Bobby is really on my list too. More at the top. I don't know who Jamie Farr is.

August 8. Dear Diary. It's much harder to see Mickey now, and I crave him all the time. I go by the butcher's after school and we kiss in the meat locker until it gets so cold I can't stand it anymore. Mickey can always stand it. He can stand anything.

Mickey went to the Marines place and signed up. They'll tell him in a couple weeks if he's in. I can't believe he's going to go. I'll miss him so much I'll die without him.

I went to Cassie's birthday party. Sweet 16. I hope I don't have a sunburn like that when I turn 16. She peeled into the cake. God, it was sick.

August 10. Dear Diary. Mickey found Bobby. They had a big fight up at the missile base. But Bobby pulled out one of his daddy's hunting rifles off the rack. Thank "God" Mickey backed down. He's brave, but he's not stupid.

August 16. Dear Diary. Oh God. Last night, we got into our first fight. He wanted to break into Kellman's and get some Ludes. I told him I didn't want to get caught because my father would kill me. He called me a PD. I couldn't believe it. I cried so hard. I could barely breathe and I thought I would faint.

He was real quiet. He didn't say anything the whole time I was crying.

Then when I stopped, he asked me if I ever fucked

Bobby! I said no "fucken" way! I never did. But I guess when he and Bobby were fighting, Bobby said I was a good "lay"! I swear to God, I'm going to kill that PD "dick". And no matter what I said, Mickey wouldn't believe me. He said he could read my spirit, waving like a flag two inches off my body, and it was a red flag warning him to stay away from deception. I cried so hard. My eyes were drained out. I told him I made out with Bobby once but we never even got to first base.

Mickey just got out of the car, walked around to my door, opened it up, and pulled me out. Then he got back in the car and drove off without a word.

August 24. Dear Diary. Bobby Gunter is a vegetable. He drowned in his mother's fish pond in the back of the house. Even though there was only an inch of water in there, they say that's all it takes. Carla says he'll be like a retarded kid the rest of his life and can't even piss. I guess it's sad, but right now, I think he deserves it. Will I go to hell for saying that?

I haven't seen Mickey since "that night", and I've cried every day it seems like, but I have my suspicions he might have done something to Bobby. Call it "womens' intuition".

I hate him. Fuck you, Mickey Knox.

August 30. Dear Diary. My father went out to his car this morning and found animal intestines all inside. He "upchucked" five or six times before he could even call the police. He told them Mickey did it, because of

Mickey working at a butcher's place and everything. I guess that makes sense.

My mother can't stop shaking.

So big news. We're moving to Talahassee. My father blames me, but he's a big piece of PD shit if you ask me. I never want to see this town or Mickey Knox again.

What a terrible summer. I hope my sophomore year is a lot better than this one, or I'm going to be really mad.

CHAPTER 5

Had Scagnetti known anything about lovers, anything about love, he wouldn't have wasted his time planning roadblocks and checkpoints to catch his prey. He simply would have headed for Las Vegas. Riding into the sunset, that's where Mickey and Mallory would be, no gamble at all.

Sprawling across the desert wasteland like stray pieces of God's Lego set, the city was absurd, a playground. Time stopped within its walls, day became night, and everything was immediate: the 7-Eleven of sin. Within this alternative universe, men who wouldn't race a yellow light suddenly found themselves $5,000 in the hole, while their schoolteacher wives played video poker and watched showgirls dance topless.

Las Vegas was a city built for true mad love. Anything less couldn't last.

* * *

They pulled into town around sundown, just in time to see the glittering neon sparkle to life.

While Mickey went to get a room, Mallory wandered by herself through the casino, past the jungle oasis, the giant fishtanks, the sports bar reggae band, and the roulette wheel. What struck her most was that there seemed to be no walls whatsoever, just paths of carpet flowers weaving through the space like Candyland, a trail that led her twice to the baccarat tables, or perhaps just once to two separate tables with identical Japanese businessmen. Signs hanging from the ceiling pointed to various destinations, but none showed you how to get out.

And everywhere—*everywhere*—there were slot machines. Lined up in rows, they stood in place while worker ants fed them with quarters over and over, eventually moving to different machines or signaling other insects for change (more food) or a drink for themselves. The slots themselves were nothing more than lights and gears; a row of dollar slots stood open as another worker collected the honey, methodically noting his progress on a clipboard.

Mallory sat herself down in the astrological theme section of the casino and played Capricorn. Mickey's birthday, not hers.

The machine was only capable of playing four notes, the same four notes from the pinball, yet all the chiming she heard in the casino was built of those same four notes, repeating and overlapping in an endless, groggy hum. With only two quarters to her name, the casino's video cameras captured Mallory as she soon won back fifteen, then lost ten. It would be days later before police would play back the scene where a string of six losses finally had her kicking the machine.

By then, the Knoxes would be long gone from Vegas, and the body count they left in their wake would rise by another twelve.

A couple of rows away, a big spender from Texas named Peter T. Rice watched as Mallory found a different machine. Called "The Tower," the three pay lines converged in a spiderweb on the face, as if the glass had been broken and pieced back together with silver tape. Mallory was the only person playing in the row, tucked back against a wall (a wall!) of mirrors that seemed to be looking into a different, emptier casino.

Rice remembered specifically how Mallory straddled the machine as she put in three quarters with each pull. "She never won big, but she always seemed to have just enough to keep going," he recalled.

He was giving her the once over, thinking she looked pretty familiar but not quite able to put the pieces together, when he noticed someone else was doing the same—a college-aged guy playing slowly at a nearby machine.

"I knew just what he was doing," said the Texan. "He was looking at the curve where her thigh met her ass. I know, 'cause I was doing the same thing.''

Switching slots, the college boy came a little closer, rubbing his fingers to get the coin grime off them. His blond hair was cut short, fraternity style. A complimentary cigar was tucked into the pocket of his oxford shirt. Suddenly he was right behind her.

"I'm sorry, did you just say something?" he asked her, an open smile on his face.

Mallory put in three quarters, pulled the handle.

The college boy set his Heineken down by her machine as he took the next stool. "I thought I heard you say my name."

"Not unless your name's Fucker," she said.

"Could be, if that's what you want." He took a draw from his beer, held it in his mouth for a long time before he swallowed.

Mallory seemed to be barely aware of the boy's presence, Rice recalled. "All her attention was on that slot machine," he said. "At least that's what I thought at the time. It was like she was trying real hard to understand how it worked."

The boy was undeterred, however. "I think you're the hottest woman in this entire casino," he said. "And I would consider it a personal honor to bring you to orgasm."

Rice smiled, and thought that this was probably the best the boy had ever delivered that line in actual field maneuvers. Not slurred a bit. Still, the girl wasn't biting.

"I would even consider reimbursing you for your professional expenses, so to speak, if that's something you require. Or do you have someone, you know, that handles reservations for you in that way?"

The Texan forgot he was trying to be discreet as he looked over and into the girl's face, just to see how she'd respond to that one. "It took a few seconds for her to register just exactly what the kid meant," he later recalled. "But suddenly the puzzled expression disappeared from her face."

Mallory lifted the Heineken from his hands and took a sizeable draw, smiling. Her eyes had a life to them that you couldn't see unless you looked dead-on, a spark deep within the dark of her eyes. Pressing the cold bottle lightly against his knee, she moved it slowly up along the inside of his thigh to his crotch, which was already stiffening. She rubbed the bottle up and down in the crease a few times, watching as his eyes went wide. Just as he was reaching to guide her hand, she gave the bottle back to him, and got up to leave.

"What's your room number, Fucker?"

"Sixteen sixty-nine," he said with a smile. "That mean you'll be coming up?"

"I haven't decided yet," she said, walking away, turning back. "But if I do, I'll bring a friend."

"Who?" he shouted, a shit-eating grin on his face.

"You'll love it," she called back, almost gone. "It'll blow your mind."

The Texan watched the boy do a little dance as the girl disappeared into the crowd. The next time he'd see the boy's face was on the nine o'clock news, after cleaning woman Connie Rodriguez discovered his naked body in room 1669 at twelve-fifteen the next afternoon, and fainted at the sight.

The coroners removed twenty-seven separate shards of green glass from the jaw of UW Madison junior Chip Burkhart during an autopsy that determined he had probably been forced to hold an empty Heineken bottle deep within his throat, in a simulation of fellatio. The bottle was then smashed with a hard object, likely the table leg found nearby, sending fragments of glass through the soft palette and into the lower brain case, also puncturing the windpipe in several areas. It was the accumulation of blood in the lungs that finally killed him.

Based upon acid stains found on nickels and quarters near the body, coroners also opened his stomach, discovering $18.75 in change, mostly quarters, but with a few dollar tokens as well. Burkhart had been forced to swallow his gambling money prior to his death, holding down much of it but vomiting on three or more occasions.

The police report speculated that the killers had played him like a slot machine.

* * *

As it turned out, Burkhart's was only the first body to be found in a series that had begun much earlier, just minutes after Mickey and Mallory had arrived in Vegas.

While his baby was down playing slots in the casino, Mickey had gone to find a room for the night. He bypassed the registration desk altogether.

Slowly cruising the hallways of the eleventh floor, he found that the door locks wouldn't respond to the usual means of picking. The room keys at the Mirage had no teeth, just magnetic stripes that activated codes in the central computer. It was enough to make you want to take some four-eyed, math-loving mama's boy and beat his fat head against the wall, thought Mickey. Frustrated that his Bowie knife was no match for modern technology (police found similar scratch marks on nine separate doors), he was headed for the elevators when he spotted a woman walking in his direction.

The woman was in her mid-forties, still slender and striking as she walked down the hallway, weaving a bit. She carried two stacks of folders in the crook of each arm. Mickey turned, pretending to be unlocking a door as she passed, watching as she fumbled with her key, the folders slipping, the lock turning, when suddenly he charged. Lifting her from behind, he pushed her into the room, a hand wrapping around her mouth to choke her scream as the door swung silently shut, locking automatically.

It only took Mickey a minute to find Mallory down in the crowded casino, wandering to the edges, in the dark quiet corners no one else would seek. Riding up in the mirrored elevator, they danced to Frank Sinatra singing "Witchcraft," Mickey's hands wrapping clear around her waist, fingers sliding past the edge of her jeans as she hiked herself up on his leg. Her nails ran through his thick wild hair, down behind his ears to the stubble on his jaw. She kissed him along the collar of his shirt, curving down into the indentation just below the Adam's apple. The "Jesus hollow," she called it, because it looked like the head of a man sitting on a throne, the collarbone forming his arms, lifted up to the sides. The hollow caught Mickey's smell, a drug to her.

Mickey carried her down the hall, her legs wrapped around his waist, kissing so hard he couldn't see right. In the room, they never broke skin contact while he peeled off her clothes and his. A flying boot left a black mark on the wall. They moved and flexed like a single muscle, yin and yang, skin sliding across skin without differentiation, inside her, between him, together. He wrapped big arms around her like a mother shielding her babies, a hold that would smother her if he weren't breathing into her as they kissed.

She pressed her hands down his back and felt him, too, down where he entered her. They were two strands of yarn, twisted together into one. Unbreakable, until their fate would begin to unravel.

Hog-tied and gagged in the closet, Liz Delacroix watched through the gap between the doors as two strangers had sex in the bed in the hotel room she was charging to the convention. Her lips were beginning to sting and swell from the adhesive soaking into her skin: three stickers reading, "Hello, my name is . . ."

Liz watched them make love for two solid hours before she blacked out.

CHAPTER

6

WAYNE: Tonight on *American Maniacs*, we're visiting with professional bodybuilders Simon and Norman Hun. Gentlemen, what do you think of Mickey and Mallory Knox?

SIMON: I admire them.

NORMAN: I do, too.

WAYNE: But how can you say that?

SIMON: They're mesmerizing.

NORMAN: Hypnotising.

SIMON: Have you seen *Pumping Iron*?

WAYNE: Yes.

NORMAN: Then you've seen the scene where Arnold Schwarzenegger is talking to Lou Ferrigno.

WAYNE: Yes.

SIMON: Through the power of a simple word—

NORMAN: —and a snake-eyed glare—

SIMON: —and a snake-eyed glare, Arnold was able to totally psych out any confidence Ferrigno had.

NORMAN: He squashed him mentally before physically defeating him.

SIMON: He had the edge. The mind's edge.

NORMAN: Mickey and Mallory have that edge.

SIMON: Only on a much grander scale.

NORMAN: They've hypnotized the nation.

SIMON: Schwarzenegger was the king of the edge before they came along.

WAYNE: You say this and yet . . . you two are both victims of Mickey and Mallory.

(The camera ZOOMS back to reveal that both Simon and Norman are in wheelchairs, their legs gone.)

SIMON: Yes.

NORMAN: Yes.

WAYNE: How can you say that you "admire" them?

NORMAN: It's like this, Wayne. Two people are standing in a dark room waiting for the other to attack. These two people can't see each other, yet they know they're there. Now, they can either stand in that dark room forever waiting until they die of boredom, or one of them can make the first move.

WAYNE: Why can't they just shake hands and be friends?

NORMAN: They can't because neither knows if the other is a deranged senseless killer like the Knoxes. So, you may as well make the first move.

WAYNE: And they made the first move?

NORMAN: Unfortunately, yes.

SIMON: But you see, that's okay, Wayne.

WAYNE: Why?

SIMON: They passed the "edge" along to us.

WAYNE: How so?

SIMON: By taking away our legs. Now we have to fight harder to get ahead than anyone else you'll find in this gym. Probably the whole city. They gave us the fighting spirit. Before this happened I was content. Now I'm pissed off. Now I'm half a man and I've got to work like the devil to get whole again.

WAYNE: But you'll never be whole again.

SIMON: Never is a very long time, Wayne. A word only the weak use. I'm not a sore loser. Even if I don't have a leg to stand on, I'm going to get up and fight this world until I'm on top again.

NORMAN: That's the Mickey and Mallory way.

SIMON: And that's the way of the world.

NORMAN: They're just shocking the world into remembering the primal law.

SIMON: Survival of the fittest.

WAYNE: One last question. Usually Mickey and Mallory kill all of their victims. Why did they let you two survive?

NORMAN: They had us tied down during one of their house raids, you've seen the headlines, and they were taking a saw to our legs before they were gonna kill us.

SIMON: Just for fun, I guess.

NORMAN: And then Mallory stops Mickey and says, "Hey, these are the Brothers Hun."

SIMON: Mickey stops sawin' on my leg and says, "Oh my God, I'm your biggest fan!"

NORMAN: Apparently, they've seen all our films.

SIMON: They were especially influenced by *Conquering Huns of Neptune*.

NORMAN: So, Mallory calls 911 and they took off.

SIMON: They actually apologized.

CHAPTER 7

When she awoke the next morning, Mallory was pissed that Mickey hadn't told her he had someone tied up in the closet.

"Taking hostages is one thing, but not telling me you got some whore watching us two in bed is just plain wrong, Mickey," said Mallory, who had just awakened her lover by prodding his chin with the barrel of his own .357 magnum.

Liz Delacroix was still trying to catch her breath, having just had the wind knocked out of her and two ribs fractured from the good kicking Mallory had delivered upon discovering her in the closet when she woke up.

Mickey's gaze was still clouded with sleep as he looked up at Mallory. Liz wondered later how much of this grogginess was sincere, and how much was just stalling for time while he came up with a good response.

"Well, you know, baby," said Mickey, struggling to find the right words, "how we decided to always leave somebody alive to tell about it every time we killed somebody?''

"Yeah? What about it?" said Mallory.

"Well . . . I figured this woman here could be a testimony to our love.''

Mallory looked at Mickey, incredulous. "She could be *what*?"

"Yeah," said Mickey, his voice growing in confidence as he slowly seemed to wake up. "I just want the whole world to know that we do more than just kill people. This woman here could be a testament to our eternal and undying love.''

Mickey looked up to see if Mallory was buying it. She wasn't *not* buying it, so he continued. "I figured if I told you she was in there, why you'd get all self-conscious and stuff and it just wouldn't seem natural.''

Mallory thought about it for a moment, almost wanting to believe it. "Really?" she said.

"Sure, baby," said Mickey. "If we killed her, nobody would ever know.''

Mallory threw herself into his arms for a reassuring hug. "There you go, baby," said Mickey, kissing her before setting her aside to get up and take a shower.

Mallory sat down on the corner of the bed and looked at Liz in the closet.

"What're you looking at!" she yelled.

Liz's mouth was still taped; there was no way for her to reply, even if she'd had something to say. Lying there in a heap, she must not have seemed like much of a threat. Because much to Liz's amazement, Mallory began to pour her heart out.

"You know, men, you just can't trust 'em, can you?" said Mallory, looking to Liz for sympathy. Stunned, Liz nodded in assent.

"I mean, most of the time, I feel like Mickey is my perfect mate, you know? I feel like everything he's thinking, I know exactly what it is. And the same goes double for him. He must know every thought that passes through my mind. Since I met Mickey, I don't want nobody else."

She paused for a moment.

"I guess it's kind of that way with women, you know?"

Liz nodded.

"So how come I didn't know he had you in the closet?" she said, her face suddenly storming over with anger. Liz began to fear for her life as Mallory stood up and began to pace the room.

"I wonder if he was thinkin' about you in there while he was making' love to me," she said. "I *hate* it when I think he's keeping secrets from me. We're not even two people. We're one soul. That's what Mickey always says. A single person divided between two bodies. How could it be that even when we're closest, even when we're lying in each other's arms, he could lie to me? Well maybe not 'lie' exactly, but you know, keep something from me."

Mallory grabbed a brush and set herself to straightening out the long hair on the blond wig she picked up off the floor, having discarded it in the throes of passion the night before. She couldn't seem to get one particular clump unknotted, and began chewing on it in aggravation.

"Mickey likes blond hair," she said sarcastically. Mallory's own hair was bottle black, straggly, and thin, which Mallory always referred to as "white girl hair." "Says it makes him feel like he has two girls to love."

Suddenly, Mallory looked over at Liz with a look of steely predation in her eye. Liz felt her heart stop with fear of the intent she saw in Mallory's visage.

"*You* have blond hair," said Mallory, looking from Liz to the wig and back again.

Liz began to pray that the sound of Mickey's shower would stop, that he would come out and make good on his promise to let her live and tell the world of their sexual exploits, which she vowed to God and Mickey she would do if only this woman would stop.

She didn't.

Mallory dropped the wig and picked up the .357 as she came slowly toward the closet.

"I got no idea what happened in here before I came in," she said. "Mickey could have grabbed you, spread you, and washed it off in five minutes if he wanted to," she said.

Liz heard the sound of the safety being removed. She began to cry.

"Any man could. Mickey Knox, cute little Mickey, he's just especially good at it. Isn't he?"

The shower kept running. The sound of Mickey's voice singing, ironically, Dwight Yoakam's "What I Don't Know" rang out from the bathroom.

He clearly wasn't coming to save her.

Mallory was inches away from the closet when suddenly a knock was heard on the room door.

Mallory stopped.

"Liz? Is that you?" said a male voice from the hallway.

"Are you Liz?" asked Mallory.

Liz nodded urgently.

"Well, let's see who's come to visit you," said Mallory, an evil smile spreading across her face.

Mallory opened the door to find Carlos Imenez, assistant manager of the Las Vegas convention center leaning heavily against the door frame, with a smug gonna-get-laid look on his face. He was surprised at the sight of Mallory behind the door.

"Where's Liz?" he asked.

"Maybe she got tired of fuckin' *waiting* for you!" said Mallory, shoving him back into the hallway, stepping out herself. She was like a tornado that suddenly dropped out of the clear blue sky, ninety-eight pounds of pure, unmitigated rage that forced him back against the far door.

"You think you can just fucking knock on the door any time you damn well please and some bitch is gonna spread her fucking legs for you?"

Liz heard Mallory scream like a banshee from the hall.

"Hey, listen, I have the wrong room!" said Carlos.

"You're fucking right you do!" said Mallory.

Liz heard him laughing in the hallway. "What, are you going to hurt me?"

Mallory connected a right to his jaw and a left to the stomach, followed in close succession by a kick to the balls and two more hits to the neck. Bowed but unbloodied, Carlos charged, sweeping her off her feet back through the door and into the room.

Liz saw Mallory hit the floor, dazed. She had heaved a sigh of urgent relief when she'd heard Carlos at the door. She'd been sleeping with Carlos for four days now and had only known this girl for the past six hours, but something inside her told her that Carlos was making a big mistake in underestimating her now.

She was right.

Carlos walked slowly into the room, letting the door close behind him. He locked it.

Sweat was starting to drip in his eyes as he watched Mallory watching him from the other side of the room.

"Now Uncle Carlos is going to teach you a lesson," he said, chortling lecherously as he removed his belt and doubled it over, cracking it for an intimidating effect.

Mallory just gave him a big, weird smile. Then charged.

Off the corner of the bed, she leaped on him like a crazed alley cat, knocking him back against the hotel TV, on which a young married couple was learning how to gamble. The mirror shattered in its frame. Mallory managed to get on his back, and dug her nails into his chest.

Carlos screamed as he tried to rip her off, but the girl only held on tighter. She caught his throat in her arm and he dropped to the floor, smashing against the dresser to try and brush her off.

She rolled a half somersault toward the door.

"Goddam bitch!" he shouted, the blood soaking through his T-shirt in circles where her talons cut in. He wiped at it, disbelieving.

Mickey Knox must have finally heard the commotion through the sound of the shower, for at the moment he ran into the room, wet and naked, just as Carlos was reaching for a chair to throw. By instinct Mickey went for the knife in his boot.

But he wasn't wearing any boots.

"Fucking stay out of this!" screamed Mallory. "He's mine!"

"Hell, baby, I can respect that," said Mickey, who moved to block the door and enjoy the spectacle.

Mallory sprang to her feet before Carlos got into range with the chair, which was far too heavy for him to wield effectively, even with his sizeable six-foot frame. He slammed it once at the foot of the bed, but Mallory was already scrambling on top of the sheets.

By pure dumb luck, he was able to grab her

around the ankle, and tried to pull her down. But Mallory had grabbed ahold of the telephone on the nightstand as he yanked her, and the cord came ripping out of the wall socket as she went sliding across the sheets.

Mallory always had one advantage in her fights—her diminutive size not only gave her tremendous agility that was difficult to combat, but it frequently caused her opponents to underestimate her.

Carlos Imenez was no exception.

Before he could land one good hit, Mallory had the cord around his neck, choking him. Liz watched with dimming hope as Mallory twisted her way behind him, digging her knees into his back, riding him like a vertical bull. He tried to shake her off again, ramming back against the wall. But Mallory wrapped both ends of the cord around one wrist, using her free hand to smash him repeatedly over the head with the telephone receiver, cracking both plastic and bone.

"That's my girl," said Mickey.

When Carlos finally collapsed, Mallory held the cord tight for a good thirty seconds, just to make sure.

Mallory crawled over to the nightstand and lit herself a cigarette.

"You think you can find a woman who kicks more ass than me, Mickey Knox, you better marry her," she said, as Carlos's body slipped off the bed with the rest of the sheets and blankets in a curled lump on the floor.

Mickey just stood there naked and smiling. Mallory tossed him the Marlboros and the lighter. He tried to strike a casual pose, smoking by the bathroom door. She laughed. So did he.

"Here's some company for you, Liz," said Mallory, as she shoved *Carlos's body into the closet with her.

Her eyes blurred from exhaustion and grief, Liz could barely move as Carlos fell on top of her in a weird parody of what they'd been planning to do at just that moment.

"Fuck you, Liz," said Mallory, shutting the door. "And your boyfriend, too."

It was shortly thereafter that Nora Hafferty opened the doors to begin setting up for the conventioneers that were due to arrive later that morning.

Except for the accent, Nora bore a striking resemblance to television chef Julia Childs—large-boned, and somewhat masculine in countenance, but graceful and motherly in all other aspects. In fact, being a mother had been her life's work, raising four pretty okay kids in the suburbs of Detroit. Now fifty-seven, she had seen the last of her children (Kelly, a dental hygienist) abandon the nest a year and a half earlier, leaving only her and her husband, Pete (engineer, retired), rattling around in their once-cozy house.

It was that maternal instinct that kicked in as she saw the waifish girl peek her head around the corner and look around the room. Nora remembered that her initial impulse had been to take the ragged child in her arms, give her a good hot meal, and tend to the cuts and bruises that seemed to cover her body.

It may have been that instinct that saved her life.

"Is this the Angel convention?" said the girl sheepishly, unsure as to whether she should enter the room or not.

"Why, yes it is," said Nora, "but it doesn't start until later in the morning. That's why nobody's here yet."

The girl seemed somewhat crestfallen. "Oh," she said.

"But you can come back," said Nora. "Things should be starting up around ten or so."

"I can't, exactly," said the disappointed young girl. "Me and my boyfriend gotta be on the road real soon."

Nora looked out into the hallway and saw a young man with wet hair kicking the carpet impatiently, hoping he wasn't the one who was beating her.

The girl thrust a small, pink brochure at Nora. "I found this in a bookstore in my hometown in Illinois," she said. "Are you the angel lady?"

Nora Hafferty was, indeed, the "Angel Lady." Her life had been changed forever the first time she had read a book entitled *Angels Among Us* by Marianne Gaines. In the Gaines model of the universe, angels were everywhere, looking out for us and keeping bad things from happening to good wholesome folk. Learning to be happy in life, to Gaines, meant building up a relationship with your personal angels, while one's conflicts could often be traced back to battling groups of angels, set against each other in the spirit world. In all, it was a fairly comfortable cosmology, "religion-lite" as the popular press labeled it, offering all the customary benefits of organized religion—security, happiness, love, with none of the troubling overhead—worship, penance, or the risk of eternal damnation.

She now published a bimonthly newsletter (*Angel Talk*) and supervised an American Online electronic forum, the fastest-growing discussion board on the service. It was one week after her interview with both *Time* magazine and *Newsweek* that she decided to launch the first national conference on angels, to be held here in Las Vegas, Nevada.

"Did you come all the way out here just for the conference?" asked Nora of the girl, who had an oddly disturbing and powerful aura around her that Nora could never recall having experienced before. Must be an angel battle worthy of Armageddon, she thought.

"Well, we're actually on our way to—well, never mind, Mickey'd get pissed off if I was to say," she said. "But the reason we came through Las Vegas is because I heard about your conference and I wanted to come. The way things have worked out, I won't be able to attend the whole thing, but I was wondering, is there anything I could take with me?"

Nora looked at her unpacked Bekins moving boxes as she tried to remember which ones held all her promotional literature. If anyone ever needed a little help with angels, this girl was it.

"Mal, hurry up, we gotta be going," said the young man in the hallway.

"Just a second, Mickey. . . ."

"Now!" he said, with a sense of urgency that made Nora feel ever the more sorry for the girl.

She rummaged through the manila folder she was carrying with notes for her lecture that afternoon, and found a brochure to give to the girl.

"Here you go, dear," she said, thrusting it into her hand.

"Thank you, Nora," said the girl, who seemed to be deeply grateful. "My name's Mallory—"

"Mal!" yelled the boy coming in and grabbing her arm and pulling her out of the conference room.

". . . and I'll always remember how nice you were to me. You know, I can see angels, Nora. Really, I can. They're all around you."

It was six-fifteen on a Friday morning. It would be hours before the police arrived with the smelling salts to question Nora, and she realized that the most transformational event of the convention, and perhaps of her entire life, had just happened.

Liz Delacroix survived the ordeal, going on to star as herself in the NBC movie of the week *Thrill Killers: Mickey and Mallory at the Mirage Hotel*. To get around network censors, concerned about the portrayal of violence on television, director Shannon Sikes staged the entire fight in slow motion, cutting away from actual body hits to closeups of Liz's reaction. One reviewer noted that the technique gave the feeling of aquatic ballet.

Several story points were changed as well. First, Carlos fought Mickey, not Mallory, because the writers felt it would be more realistic. Second, Carlos was made white, promoted to convention center manager, and given a diamond ring with which he had planned to ask Liz for her hand in marriage. Third, the fight lasted for three and a half minutes in the movie, while in truth it was all over in less than sixty seconds.

The proper time frame was known from the original testimony of Liz Delacroix and fellow guests Ron and Martha Kuhlmann in room 1142, who watched and listened to part of the fight in the hallway through their peephole. The Milwaukee couple later told police that they hadn't reported the incident to the management because they believed it was simply a lovers' quarrel between Carlos and Mallory. Interviewed for this book, Martha confessed she actually believed Carlos was Mallory's pimp, and that the disagreement had been over money or drugs. She hadn't wanted to say that earlier, because she was trying to be more positive and openminded about things at the time, having flown out to Las Vegas for a three-day convention on angels.

CHAPTER
8

The odds are we will never know which route Mickey and Mallory took upon leaving Las Vegas that night, a journey that would eventually lead them to Gallup, New Mexico, two days and six hundred miles later. While at least eight small-town gas-station owners claim to have been visited by the couple during these "lost days," their statements were largely dismissed at the time by FBI and state police as publicity hoaxes when the owners failed to provide the most basic details, like the make of the car, Mallory's scorpion tattoo or their accents (Arkansas for Mickey, Illinois for Mallory). Pete Bucane of the Pump-n-Go in Juniper, Arizona, for instance, had already called in an order for three hundred and fifty printed T-shirts ("Mickey and Mallory: What a Gas") to his brother-in-law, Stan, when he called the sheriff's to report the couple's visit.

According to receipts later found in his Geo Metro, Owen Traft of Palo Alto, California, would be one of the first to buy a Mickey and Mallory T-shirt.

Extra large.

Although there are few witnesses to track their whereabouts during those two days, the killers themselves provide a strangely effective journal of this period, in the form of the "angel workbook" given to Mallory by Nora Hafferty (who incidentally wrote the questions). Recovered from the glove compartment of the Challenger, the workbook offers some insight into the story of her "wedding" to Mickey, her sexually abusive father, and her jealousy when it came to other women.

Based upon the two murders known to have occurred in Gallup, we can surmise that Mallory wrote her answers on two consecutive days of travel, completing roughly half the pamphlet each day. Indeed, the ink changes from black to red after the sixth question, the likely split between days, as does the tone of her response. Several of the questions and answers are included below.

In Marianne Gaines's book *Angels Among Us,* she describes the concept of an "angel quest," in which a person actively seeks to identify and communicate with these forces in his or her life. Where are you now on your "angel quest?"

We're on a road going to New Mexico. Mickey is driving. He's been driving since we left Las Vegas, that was about four hours ago. He says we're in

Arizona, not New Mexico yet, but we'll get there. I don't see any angels here but Mickey, who I think is an angel, but is probably not what this is supposed to be. If it means that we're looking for angels, then I think we'll find them when we get to New Mexico. I am on my angel quest now with Mickey. He doesn't know as much about this though. I keep it secret, even though I love him, but it looks like now we have secrets from each other so this is mine. So there Mickey Knox!

Do you believe angels are actual incarnate beings, or are they simply shorthand for concepts like love and luck?

Yes I think angels have a lot to do with love. Mickey & me just got married maybe an hour ago (I'm MALLORY KNOX and don't you forget it!) and I could feel stuff all around us. It was just Mickey and me on this bridge over the prettiest canyon I ever saw, and I mean it, it was like heaven. Mickey said something about God and souls and something, then cut my hand and his and we squoze our hands together. These couple of drops of blood fell like a mile down to the river, and I remember thinking that sooner or later that blood would go to all the oceans of the world and maybe someday when I was like 80 (ha! I'll be dead!) I would be drinking lemonade and in there would be a little blood from Mickey and me getting married. He got these rings for each of us, two silver snakes all coiled around each other.

I was wearing this piece of cloth I stole off a table at

the conference as a veil (it was long!) and just as we finished kissing, the wind came and blew it off. It fell down into the canyon too but really slow, like it was flying. Like it was an angel floating down from heaven. If someday I found it again down there (where?), I would want to be buried in it wrapped up like a mummy in our love.

What is your religous background? Did you attend church regularly? Do you consider yourself a religious person?

My mom, my dad, my brother and me all went to St. Andrew's until I was maybe twelve. I remember it was pretty with the music and the choir and Jesus hanging there naked. I remember thinking he was pretty. He's a lot bigger than Jesus was but Mickey reminds me of him when he's sleeping sometimes, his arms out on the bed like he's falling into a big thing of iced tea.

One Sunday dad said he wasn't going to church that day and then he never went again. I was like twelve or thirteen when he said I couldn't go anymore either because he didn't want me flirting with boys at church. Like I was giving them head when I knelt down to pray. Mom was a total pussy and didn't fight him on it so it wasn't long that he started fooling with me on Sundays when they were at church, mostly just getting him off but eventually he wanted more. The first few times it happened I just switched off like a light and when it was over I felt shitty but it wasn't like I was there. But then one day I didn't turn off and while he was down there started thinking about Jesus and how he was hung up for like a week and how this only lasted maybe an hour. So it really couldn't compare. And it was funny like by the next week my taste had changed, I swear, and he couldn't eat it anymore. (I never told Mickey about this, but he thinks I'm the best, so unless he's doing any comparison shopping that I don't know about I won't ask.) He couldn't get stiff because of his heart medicine which I know pissed him off so he might dabble a little, but by fourteen or fifteen it was next to nothing. He'd talk about fucking me, calling me a whore or a cunt or whatever, but he was all talk because it just wasn't going to happen.

My mother was pretty religious until we killed her but I think she knew about what he was doing almost the whole time so she's probably damned to Hell, which is fine by me.

———

Have you ever experienced an incident where you felt an angel take control of your body?

When people start making trouble for Mickey and me there's this funny feeling, like I want them to be even bigger dicks to me because I know it will get me mad and suddenly like wonder woman BOOM! I can just go off on them. I don't know how I do it sometimes. It just feels natural, like someone else who is really good at kicking the shit out of people is there to tell me how. You can't just go all nuts crazy even if you're strong like Mickey. I'm not, so I have to hit in just the right places and I do. I don't know why, I just

do. So this angel, I guess it's an angel, helps me
do that.

———

Give your angel companion a name. Don't think
too long—soon you'll be able to know his or her
name yourself!

Farrah.

———

Is your angel companion male, female, or asexual?

Farrah is a girl like me but she's mega-tough, and
has pretty blonde hair. She could kick any guy's ass,
even Mickey's if she had to. But I don't let her
because I love Mickey, even though if I was her I
would probably want to sometimes. Farrah couldn't
be a guy because if he was, he would have gone after
Mickey for being such a fucker. I wouldn't have been
able to stop him, because you can't control men when
they get mad. Mickey Knox, for example.

I think maybe I am his angel. I do a lot of angel
things, like protect him and watch his back, sing him
to sleep and really he probably wouldn't be here if it
weren't for me loving him when he went to prison for
stealing my dad's car. He said while he was there he
dreamed about me every night, and I dreamed about
floating over him, so that's something. Also before he
met me he was never sweet with anyone at all—he
used to kill kittens even, so I brought out the good in
him which is an angel thing to do, I bet. But I don't
think he has anyone like Farrah floating around him,
just me. He would be a total psycho without me, and
you better realize it, Fucker!

We're pulling in to get Mickey some food (pie) so I'll be right back.

———

Do you believe animals have angels, or can become angels?

Fuck if I know.

———

Have you ever been angry at your angels?

So last night cute little Mickey decides we need us a new hostage DONT ASK ME WHY and picks some little high school whore to tie up in the corner of the room while he tries to get in me and the thing is I CAN TELL he's looking at her—FUCKER not like I'm fucking blind. So I tell him he can be cute little Mickey all by himself and I go smoking and driving almost just driving away for good, swear to God. Fucker!

Then at this gas station last night I think ha ha ha Mickey Knox, if you can, so can I godamnit. And the gas guy is going down on me when he says, you're Mallory Knox, ain't you, and he starts to freak out. MOTHERFUCKER!

———

Have angels ever helped find something that you lost?

Cute little Mickey doesn't know it but we're lost right now, turned off the road when the state trooper was behind us. Onto a smaller road, then a smaller road. I KNOW he's going to say its my fault I KNOW he is and it isn't at all. We were off the map before I even said left but he wasn't thinking of how to get rid of the cop so ONCE AGAIN I had to do all the thinking which pisses me off. It's MY FAULT we're lost it's MY FAULT we're in indian country it's MY FAULT his daddy blew his head off with a shotgun when he was little. Did he? Hey now, maybe you wonder. Cute little Mickey with a big old gun. Then again, if I had a little shit like Mickey, I'd kill myself too.

CHAPTER
9

The following chapter is excerpted from Jack Scagnetti's *Born to Die,* a never-published account of the Knox case which he was writing at the time of his death. In truth, *not* writing would be the better description; sources at the publishing house confirm that pages were slow in coming, and that the book had been pushed off schedule at least three separate times.

There was no clear consensus on the reason for the delays. A former executive assistant claimed that a parade of well-respected ghost writers were brought in to work with Scagnetti, but each left the project after less than a week of work, either by choice or by force. None of the writers the assistant named would confirm or deny their involvement with the project, although Doug Workman, who shadowed Scagnetti on *Supercop* admitted that he was contractually prohibited from discussing *Born to Die.*

"It sounds like a good title for a book, though,

doesn't it?" he said in a telephone interview, with a sly smile you could perceive through the receiver. "I'm sure if there was a book by that title, it would be fascinating."

In fact there was a book by that title, at least a hundred and ten pages of it, as two different readers at the publisher have confirmed. According to them, the early pages were classic Scagnetti, a poor man's James Ellroy. However, the writing became darker and less coherent as the pages became less frequent. One reader described sections as "dense and ironic, some sort of shorthand for evil"; while another reader asked to be removed from the project, claiming that it was causing her nightmares. Yet both readers agree that whole sections of the book were being pulled toward the end, never sent down for any verification or coverage. Sue Berger, Scagnetti's editor, refused all requests to be interviewed, stating in a fax only that "plans for a book on Mickey and Mallory Knox have been cancelled. The untimely death of Jack Scagnetti was not a factor in this decision."

One irony which makes this web of denial specifically sticky is that the publisher had in fact already sent out advance copies of one Scagnetti chapter to leading national magazines, hoping for a presale to help hype the launch. Sources suggest that Berger herself was largely responsible for doctoring the pages that went out, nervous about her holding her corporate foothold with her one ace-writer missing his deadline. Following

Scagnetti's death, Berger personally called to get those advance chapters back from the magazines, but photocopiers ran wild, especially when it was announced that the book was cancelled. Jaded New Yorkers who had never read a Scagnetti book before, suddenly found themselves reading the chapter strictly for its novelty sake.

The hippest thing Jack Scagnetti ever wrote was posthumous.

By special arrangement with the publisher, we reprint the chapter here as it falls into our story. Minimal changes have been made, editing a few points for clarity only.

From *Born to Die*
BY JACK SCAGNETTI

The call came in at eight-forty-five in the A.M. Twenty minutes, six cups of coffee and half a pack of Kools later, I pulled onto the Las Vegas strip and ditched the unmarked.

Destination: The Mirage.

Some blonde and her Mex boyfriend had been dumped in the closet by the dynamic duo only hours before. The maid from the morning shift who'd opened the door thought she'd walked in on them doing it in the closet 'til she saw the blood.

Instantly the place was crawling with local homicide on a room-to-room. Bingo: stiffs everywhere.

The buzz was starting to kick in as I walked through the casino. Row after row of suckers slugging in their pension plans one quarter at a time. The place was a live-capture trap. Silicone boobs, neon lights, and the promise of big, easy money lured 'em in; nothing let 'em out.

A couple of local uniforms were posted at the elevator on the sixteenth floor. They jumped like two raw nerves when the elevator doors opened and I walked out. Even in a town like Vegas, M&M's playtime aftermath could still make a twenty-year badge go hinky at the sight.

I flashed my I.D. They backed off.

The room: courtesy Hurricane Mickey. Blood-stained quarters at the foot of the bed. Empty Heinekens. Broken chair leg. The toe tag was a kid named Chad Burkhart. No sign that he put up any kind of a fight; must've known he was fucked, never clued in on just how bad 'til ol' Mick took a chair leg to his larynx.

Flash: the kid with his hands on Mallory. Smell the rage, the fear. Mickey Knox, he was one jealous son-of-a-bitch.

Down to floor eleven. Even without Miss Wyoming, I knew Mallory had killed the Mex herself. Claw marks, phone cord, the way a ninety-eight-pound chick fights a big man. Mickey probably waatched as she choked the life out of the poor bastard. Probably got a hard-on, and why not? Any dame who could kill a man twice her weight bare-handed deserved that kind of salute.

Before the lab boys confiscated the Mirage linen, I sniffed around.

His pillowcase: dirty, oily hair. Needed a shower.

Hers: honey-sweet, hair washed in apples.

The wet spot on the bed was dry now. Mickey was

there, but mostly it was sweet Mallory. I knew I'd always remember that scent.

I left the bag-and-tag to the morgue boys. Already the bodies were beginning to bloat. For me, it was back to the road. Back to the chase. If I'd had the time, I would have stayed to watch 'em wheel out the stiffs through the casino, just for laughs. Would it be enough to make the blue-hairs raise their gaze from the slots?

Maybe so. But probably not.

Six minutes over the New Mexico border. Nothing but tumbleweeds and scorpions for miles. But the air is thick with Mickey and Mallory.

They've been here. Gut jitters and the throb of blood in my temples never lie. Boom, boom boom. Scagnetti sonar.

The cellular rings. Katherine Ginniss, tired of brain busting at Quantico. Calling to bust my balls.

"You've got only half the number of roadblocks you need for California," she says. I can hear the sound of paper shuffling in the background. "They could get through without even consciously avoiding the inter-cept sites. We have to at least target *B* and *C* roads."

I took a long, slow drag off my Kool—how many has it been? My hundredth?

"California ain't where they're headed, Kathy."

"Don't pull that patronizing cop shit on me, Scag-netti. Every sign says they're headed west. They have a diurnal travel pattern, textbook outlaw obsession and—Jesus Christ!—twenty-three bodies strung along a very clear east-west path. Don't tell me they sud-denly pulled a U-turn."

It wasn't that I hated Katherine Ginniss. Hell, under other circumstances we might even have been pals. She was a star in the Quantico think tank, a Harvard shrink who profiled Gacy, Manson, and a half dozen other people you never heard of. I never heard of. Amateur beat-offs who were pulled off the streets before they could kill once—the immunization theory of criminal justice. A hard line to defend from the ivory tower.

But when people asked me what I thought of the FBI—and they did—I said it was like making a science out of fucking a woman. Sure, you could measure it, photograph it, tape record it; try it this way, against the wall, in a car, on the bed; and wire it up and count the number of goddamn neural impulses. But in the end, either you could fuck or you couldn't, and a hundred years of clinical study couldn't change that.

Bottom line: Katherine Ginniss couldn't catch a real pro if he was right under her nose. And I knew that for a stone-cold fact.

I pulled out my sunglasses. The hard New Mexico light was beginning to burn. Put a smile in my voice. Ol' Jack, you charmer.

"Roadblocks aren't for them," I said. "That's not where they're headed."

"If they make it to Los Angeles, or even the Valley, it will be carnage," she said. An edge to her voice. Trying to make an asshole like me hear what she's saying. "The only reason the body count was so low in Las Vegas was that no one was seen as a threat. People were too busy losing money to cause them any trouble. Picture what's going to happen if they hit Los

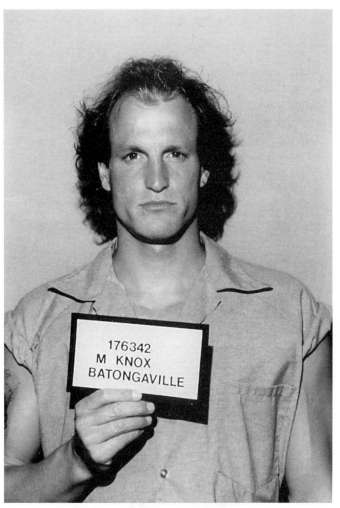

Portrait of a killer.

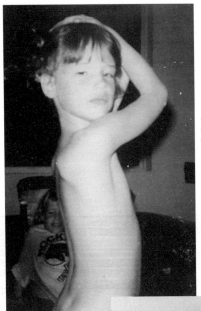

Mallory,
the vamp.

Mallory Knox:
Prisoner #76845

76845
M KNOX
BATONGAVILLE

The Wilsons: a typical American family.

Mickey Knox's 1970 Dodge Challenger 383
Magnum RT convertible.

Randall Krevnitz,
sole survivor of the Kankakee Sonic
parking lot massacre.

Site of Gerald Nash's death outside
Alfie's Donut Shop.

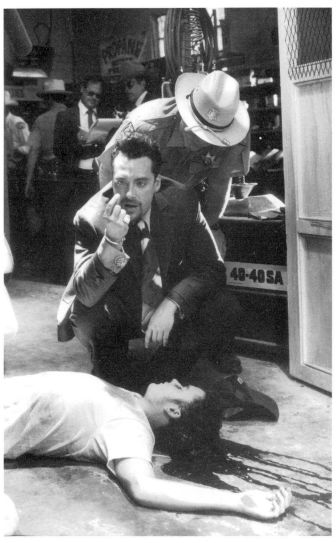

"Jimmy Lupont was found with his fly
unbuttoned, a bullet in his forehead. I opened his
mouth–a pubic hair stuck between his teeth."
–From *Born to Die* by Jack Scagnetti

Wayne Gayle, host of *American Maniacs*,
reporting live from the Knox trial.

Mickey in chains.

M&M: the craze and the crazed.

Dwight McClusky, warden of Batongaville Prison,
knew Mickey and Mallory were trouble
from the start. But even he couldn't have
predicted what lay ahead.

Angeles. They're stars. Their press is out of control. Everyone's going to try and be a hero; everyone is going to want a piece of Mickey and Mallory. And once it starts, they will not stop killing until they're killed. That city is Chernobyl for serial killers. We can't risk them getting through.''

Crushed my cigarette into the ashtray that was already flowing over with butts. ''Add one hundred units. Use my name, whatever it takes,'' I said.

Silence. Took her by surprise. Thought she had won. Thought that it mattered.

The roadblocks weren't for them. They were for her. And Joe Barbecue in Ojai who wanted to tuck his baby girl into bed and think he was safe. Which was nothing but a big, fat lie. Right at that moment he was being hunted from a hundred different directions— Mick and Mal were the least of his problems. There were hinges snapping on every corner. Guys who'd toed the line for fifty years and suddenly couldn't take it anymore. Most dangerous of all: Joe Barbecue himself. Any second he could slip into that dark side, snap the neck of that baby girl, thrill to the sound of the air being choked out of his wife while they made love. There were not enough roadblocks in the world to catch all the evil floating out there, waiting.

It was open season on humans.

I was only four hours behind Mickey and Mallory by the time I reached the Two Forks Diner outside of Buttfuck, New Mexico. The scene was familiar, but the blood was fresher. They were close.

Scorpions dancing at the edge of the road. I pulled

in to the sight of a stiff outside in the gravel, a knife between the shoulder blades, shards of window glass shattered across his back. Only one possibility—the knife had been thrown from the inside, shattered the window, then plugged the poor bastard. An impossible trajectory.

But then, that was Mickey Knox.

The only survivor: a trucker named Townsend. Stared dead ahead as he spoke, like he could still see the Challenger roaring into the desert.

Mallory snatched the quarters from the charity jar to feed the juke box: Robert Gordon. Started snake dancing to the rockabilly, a she-devil in red hip-huggers and suede boots.

Early Hickey, a lonesome trucker who stopped to soak up the Millers on his twice-weekly runs to Denver, thought he had a chance with Mallory. Thought any bimbo dancing solo in a halter-top would be just dyin' to ride ol' Earl in the back of the Peterbilt. Townsend said he couldn't remember what it was Earl said that made Mallory stop dancing.

And start kicking his ass.

One-two to the jaw. Earl's laughing. A knee to the groin and he's grabbing his nuts. A kick in the head and he's over the Formica. Bang, into the table. Bang, into the window.

"How sexy am I now, motherfucker!" yells Mallory, cracking his neck. Catsup, mustard, Mallory chanting L-7 lyrics, "You made my *Shitlist* . . ." Riot Girl from hell.

Earl ain't laughin' anymore.

Mickey Knox, cool as a cuke, finished his pie and

milk, stopping to kill Earl's buddy when he tried to cut in on Mallory's action. One, two, three cuts with a Bowie knife. Then the cook—one shot to the forehead, brains splattered across the back wall. Then the waitress—tried to block a bullet with a coffeepot. That left Townsend, the only one they didn't send to the happy hunting ground.

"When them people ask you who did this, you tell 'em Mickey and Mallory Knox did it, all right?" said Mal.

They weren't only living their own legends, they were writing them.

By now, I knew Mickey and Mallory were unraveling. They were covering fewer miles, not real direction. Hungry wolves wandering the desert. I holed up in a cheap motel, waiting for them to strike again, passing time with the local girls and a bottle of Wild Turkey.

Didn't have to wait long.

Seventeen-year-old Jimmy Lupont had showed up for work at the Camel Rock Unico at six P.M. sharp, ready to spend the late shift packing the bearings on his '68 'Vette. The job was almost done by ten o'clock when trouble pulled in for a full tank of super unleaded.

A red Challenger. Driven by Mallory Knox.

No witnesses except the security camera, perched high in the office window. Sweeping right and left in long passes. Jimmy probably knew the camera was there; thought about how it would be to play the tape for his friends after it was all over and nobody believed the story about the long-legged blonde in the muscle car who drove in for a fill-up and begged him for it on the hood of the 'Vette. Thought about jacking himself off in the La-Z-Boy after his parents had gone to bed.

The deputy on the scene had cued up the footage by the time I got there. Grainy black-and-white, no sound. But you didn't need to be a lip reader to figure out what happened.

Jimmy Lupont was found with his fly unbuttoned, a bullet in his forehead. Stretched out on the pavement, his blood mingling with the oil from the crankcase.

Saliva drops on the 'Vette. The smell on the turquoise metal-flake paint: pure Mallory. I opened his mouth—a pubic hair stuck between his teeth. He was a good-looking kid, who probably got laid a lot.

But never so hard.

But why was Mallory by herself? Where was Mickey?

Playing in his own sandbox, as it turned out. Another hostage, girl name of Elly Maisel. Trailer-park trash, same as Mickey. She survived her night at Knox Scary Farm. Just barely.

When they found her in a drainage culvert under County Road 5, her face had swollen up to where she couldn't breathe through her nose. The ambulance men tried to hold her down; that just made it worse. She pulled an arm out of its socket trying to get free. Thirteen stitches sewed up the bite she took out of one of the cops.

She was a fighter, that one; maybe that's why she lived.

I finished two cigarettes as they loaded her up. Flash: lightning. One-Mississippi, two-Mississippi, three. *Boom*. A rumble from God announcing the chance of rain. I knew Mallory was nearby, counting too. I could hear it.

What was happening to their storybook romance? The sky wasn't the only thing that was storming over. Mickey was a star now. Like all stars, he wanted to spread it around. The tape of Mallory and the gas station kid: she's scared, vulnerable.

Whatever the cause, I knew they'd start making mistakes. Real soon.

By now, they'd been forced to secondary roads. Maybe even gravel. The beauty of the desert, from a lawman's perspective, is that there aren't a dozen highways criss-crossing. Close four roads, you limit them to a hundred-mile radius. The web gets smaller.

To get around me, they'd have to go into Indian country. They might—but something told me they wouldn't last long. Something about that land that just doesn't set right. The laws of nature just don't apply. A kind of watching, a towering fear that something was there that could kick your ass permanently.

Mickey and Mallory were starting to uncoil. That place could twist them apart for good.

Twenty miles outside of Gallup, a dead bicyclist on the highway. One blast from a moving car. Neon-bright Spandex made him a great target. Still, it was pretty good shooting. He'd been down less than an hour—I drew my net tighter. A ring circling the city, with me at the center.

No doubt about it. Mickey Knox, you'll meet Jack Scagnetti tonight, you bastard.

Every lawman west of El Paso congregated in Gallup that night. Waiting for the call. Radios cross-linked and jumpy with hair-trigger operators. Domestic disturbance drew seven squad cars. Shotguns loaded. For a teenager playing his stereo too loud.

Geek cop in residence—every department has one—devised a way to switch every stoplight in the city over to red in the event of a high-speed chase. But this wasn't a car-chase movie. It was the Alamo. And ol' Jack Scagnetti was gonna be the last man standing.

I was burning up with friction. All the Wild Turkey in the world couldn't take the edge off. I passed a few hours with a little girl from the local bowling alley, but even she couldn't put out the fire. I began to roam the city like a rabid, mangy dog.

I finally parked myself in a Naugahyde booth at Grampa Grand's diner. Two hours of coffee, cigarettes, and small talk. All the time, the buzz getting louder. Like a station on the radio that was just out of tune. All you hear is static, a snatch of music now and then.

The closer I got, the more music I heard.

Ginniss called from the road. Still two hundred miles out. Disagreed about the reservation; said outlaws would see it as sanctuary from the law. *Nothing can protect them tonight,* I wanted to say. Not from me. Tonight, I'm unbeatable.

Suddenly, I felt it.

It was that radio tuning in, the buzz hitting its peak. I slid out of the booth. Punched off the phone. Stood there frozen for a good ten seconds, cold to the bone. My finger drumming on the table. I couldn't stop it. I looked around—everyone at the diner staring at me, like I was some nigger crackhead freak.

They were casting shadows on the wall. Everyone was. Bright light hanging from the center of the room, floating, its beam sweeping in a circle like a lighthouse. Shadows swinging behind them as they passed.

Only nobody sees the light except me.

Then I see one guy in the back booth. He moves his hands in front of his face. Watching the shadow fall across his eyes. He could see it, too. But no one else. I I.D. him fast: forty, balding, wearing a goddamn Mickey and Mallory T-shirt. Looking past the light, he shouts at me. I don't know what he's shouting. But I know it's time to leave.

My shadow came, too.

I'm driving without knowing it. I don't remember starting the car, or leaving the parking lot. I'm just driving. I'm getting better. It's gonna be okay. I don't know Gallup from Egypt, but the streets run straight and empty.

In my head, I'm able to sort out some of it. The volume had been turned up to ten on every sense. I couldn't turn it down. But I could ignore it. I was at the center of the web, exactly where I had placed myself. Now somebody had wandered into my trap.

Without realizing it, I was finding them. Following

their thread. The call came in on the radio—silent alarm tripped at 1500 Hayworth. A twenty-four-hour pharmacy called the Drug Zone. No shit.

I was there before I even knew it. A silent opera of black-and-whites, guns drawn, lights flashing. A horseshoe around the only entrance. I drew my gun as I walked. Might've shot my way into the store if someone hadn't pressed a megaphone into my hand. But before I could say a thing—

Mallory Knox. Came tripping through the automatic door, her skin nine shades paler than white. Didn't see the cops until it was too late. Wild dogs, they were. All over her like flies on shit. Took five of them wrestling her to the pavement, and she was still kicking like a wildcat.

I dragged her to the door, her screaming like a banshee, "Kill 'em all, kill 'em all."

Drawing my knife, I grabbed her firm around her naked belly, my fingers catching the edges of her belt, dipping in below. Could have looked like I was just trying to keep her standing. I wasn't.

"Fuck you." She spit in my face. She was green with snake-bite venom, her legs swollen at the ankles, but could still kick the shit out of a man twice her size.

But not me. Into the megaphone: "Mickey Knox! This is Jack Scagnetti, I got your wife here with me!" Around me, cops rechecking their rifles. Taking aim. "I'll cut her if you don't come out. I'll do it! I'll cut her tits off, Mickey!"

From inside, Mickey: "I'll get her a set of silicone implants, Scagnetti!" But I wasn't buying it. He was scared.

"Don't do it, baby!" shouted Mallory, biting my hand.

"I mean it!" I said. Didn't think it. Didn't plan it. But the knife grazed across her ribs. She started to bleed.

Inside, Mickey was crouched behind the checkstand for cover. No where to run. Part of me felt sorry for him—the only thing he gave a shit about was in my hands, out of his reach.

"All right, I'm coming out!" shouted Mickey. Threw down his gun, put up his hands. Cops all over him. Don't underestimate Mickey Knox, you stupid bastards, I want to yell—I don't have the chance. Quick as a rattlesnake, he's put out an eye.

They want to kill him. They can smell cop-killer blood. But a Japanese TV crew is on the scene—I don't want to make this cocksucker into Rodney King. Besides, he's mine.

They hit him with the taser guns, wires sparking against the bare skin under his motorcycle jacket. The third jolt took him down. Then every jangled nerve in the entire New Mexico sheriffs' department came unleashed on his body. Nightsticks. Motorcycle boots. Twelve broken ribs and a concussion later, they finally let him up.

Mallory was taking her own beating, her cries scraping against the sky until she just couldn't scream anymore. There was no fight left in her as I led her to the car. She just sang to herself in a low, hoarse whisper the old Nancy Sinatra song,

"These Boots Are Made for Walking."

CHAPTER
10

The crowd outside the Cook County Courthouse began gathering in the rain at 3:30 that morning, anticipating the arrival of Mickey and Mallory Knox.

Seats for the event itself had already been assigned by lottery, members of the press taking sixty of the available seventy-five seats. In accordance with recent Supreme Court opinion that the average American should have access to attend legal proceedings in person, a stipulation made to reflect the growing prevalence of *CourtTV,* the remainder of the seats were made available to the general public. In order to be eligible for the drawing, concerned citizens had to show up in person at the county registrar's office at least four weeks in advance and fill out form DR-47 in triplicate, showing both a current driver's license and proof of address. In the three years the system had been in place, the most requests sixty-year-old Dolores McGuire had processed was 239, for the high profile murder of socialite Buffy Hamsted.

For the Knox trial, the total was 3,782. Dolores McGuire quietly announced her retirement.

Police initially tried to disperse the onlookers, but by 7:00 A.M. they were forced to begin erecting barricades to block off the estimated 5000 spectators. The crowd was a cross section of America—a Charles Kurault moment—but the ones to watch were the Mickey and Mallory fans, "Generation Axe" as *Details* magazine had taken to labeling them. Ranging in age from fourteen to thirty, they were a subculture united only by look and attitude. For women, it meant hip-huggers and halter-tops, temporary tattoos applied with precision. The first wave bleached their hair, but the true cognoscenti went for the wigs, the overwhelming demand pushing prices over $700. Men had more clothing options, although without the right physique, biker-tough often came off looking amiably *Happy Days*. True believers adhered to the legend that Mickey wore his wife's underwear; indeed, the Calvin Klein fall collection picked up the trend and rode a wave of publicity after its first billboards appeared.

For those without the body or desire to emulate their idols, there were always T-shirts. Among the designs worn or available that day at the courthouse:

- An unlicensed drawing of a wild-eyed Mickey Mouse with a gun. The tagline read, WHY? BECAUSE I HATE YOU.
- A still from the cult film *Super Killers*, an animated Japanese short featuring an obscenely muscular Mickey and voluptuous Mallory.

- Parody artwork for a film called *The Dying Game*.
- A Roy Lichtenstein imitation, with Mallory looming over the barrel of a giant revolver. Her speech balloon read, NO, MOM! YOU TAKE OUT THE GARBAGE!!
- A black-and-white bull's-eye target. The back read, KILL ME NOW.

His show *American Maniacs* now consistently ranked at the top of the Nielsen's, Wayne Gale had been asked by the network to cover the event live for their morning newscast, but Wayne said no. In fact, his exact words (according to an intern who claimed to have overheard the conversation) were "Not if I was fucking made of cheese would I speak two words on that new-hope-for-bladder-control-disorder show." The network backed down—they were backing down a lot when it came to Wayne these days—and promised him a ten-thirty slot to recap the day's events.

Cutting his way through the crowd, Wayne took his place at the head of the receiving line. He checked his teeth and hair in the small mirror Julie carried with her. Pinching his nose shut, he sang a nasally chord progression to warm up the vocal cords, then flubbered his lips to get them loose. Scott, the cameraman, who'd cleaned Wayne's spit off the lens more times than he cared to remember, quickly pointed away.

"Today's the day I'm going to make a change," said Wayne, talking to Scott, or perhaps Julie, but looking straight into the camera, which was recording. "Today, no more of the hypocrisy, judging one man by his actions and another by his inaction. Christ, never! I say that I was born free and I will die free. I shall live the life I choose to live. Love who I choose to love. Freely and without consequence. Free! Free! Free! They'll never hold me down, never again!"

"Wayne, are you gay?" asked Scott.

"No! I'm alive! And I'm horny! Give me a kiss, Julie." He landed a slobbery kiss on her cheek, which she wiped off with the edge of her notepad. "Record this, Scott: Today's the day Wayne Gale stopped being a pussy. We'll put that in the show. It's honest, it's human. It's Oprah swearing the weight's off for good. I will get laid! Frequently!"

Julie was about to seek cover when the crowd suddenly shifted, crushing her up against Wayne and Scott. Lights flashing, two more squad cars escorted a plain brown sedan, the first arrival of the day.

Eighteen-year-old Grace Mulberry was the lone survivor of Mickey and Mallory's "slumber party massacre," and the prosecution's star witness. Despite overwhelming physical evidence and surveillance camera footage, District Attorney Wanda Bisbing felt she needed a victim's voice to describe the horror of the Knox attack, and Grace was the only survivor willing to testify once word leaked that Mickey Knox would be acting as his own defense. She would have to face him in cross-examination.

(In fact, it was later found that Dodge enthusiast Randall Krevnitz, the only survivor of the assault on the Kankakee Sonic, was also willing to testify. However, after several meetings with the boy, Bisbing removed his name from the list, concerned that his testimony seemed to actually support the killings.)

Grace Mulberry, however, made an ideal witness. She was the pretty, Methodist girl-next-door who had survived a terrible ordeal.

It had all begun less than half an hour after the original Sonic slayings, with Grace and her best friend Katie Hoyle arriving back at the Mulberry house, loaded down with Cokes and cheeseburgers. Her brother, Tim, and five other friends were laying out the sleeping bags, cuing up the *Rocky Horror Picture Show,* and getting ready for a night of wholesome horseplay.

That was, until Mickey and Mallory crashed the party.

"Miss Mulberry! Are you afraid to testify against Mickey Knox?" asked one reporter, stuffing a microphone into her face.

"Did you watch your friends being killed?" asked another.

"Did he rape you?"

"Do you find Mickey attractive?"

"Are you going to accept the CBS offer?"

Grace darted her head in the direction of each question, but didn't answer. Wanda Bisbing held on to her tightly, afraid the girl would lose her resolve in the face of this media assault. Behind the police lines Mickey and Mallory's fans were screaming "Fuck the bitch up!" "Traitor!" and "You should've died, you cunt!"

She was hoping Grace didn't hear.

Wayne managed to work himself through the gauntlet of police, getting the microphone in front of Grace's mouth.

"How does it feel to be the only survivor of Mickey and Mallory's reign of terror?" he asked, his Australian twang particularly edged.

"Okay," she said, frightened. Wayne had hoped for more, but the police were sweeping her up the final steps and out of his reach.

Not to fear—the main attractions had arrived. Wayne heard the crowd surge just as Grace disappeared through the courthouse doors. He turned around to see an armored police van pull up in front of the courthouse steps.

A chant of "We love Mickey! We love Mallory!" rose from the fan contingent, who began throwing M&M candies high in the air, like rice at a wedding. The candy rain fell down in all colors except brown: Legend had it that Mickey hated brown.

With megaphones, cops ordered the crowd to back away, and to stop throwing things. A skinny blond sophomore from Northwestern shouted "Fuck the pigs!" at the top of her Marlboro lungs, but aside from a momentary stir, she was not able to lead an organized revolt. She was subsequently arrested and her parents impounded her gold card.

As he unlocked the van door, Sergeant George

Kipcitz felt a sudden wave of panic. The door swung open to reveal Mickey and Mallory chained separately, handcuffs linked to waist belts linked to leg irons. It would be impossible for them to get anywhere on foot, each step limited to exactly sixteen inches. Even then, a different chain hooked them to four police officers each, threading through both cuffs and belt like a steel spiderweb. They'd pretty much have to kill them all to make a break.

It's not impossible, thought Kipcitz to himself as the guards hooked themselves on. *Anything's possible with Mickey and Mallory Knox.*

Despite the chains, Mickey managed to give a *Tonight Show* wave to the crowd as he stepped out of the van. Fans cheered enthusiastically.

"We love you, Mickey!" shouted a heavyset forty-year-old woman and her highschool daughter, who held a sign saying MURDER ME, MICKEY! The mother wore a T-shirt saying MICKEY MADE ME DO IT.

"Mallory, I wanna fuck you!" was the cry from a Pi Kap fraternity brother as Mrs. Knox was helped from the van. Her jet-black hair was cropped short.

"Okay, fuck you!" she shouted back with a big, weird smile. The crowd ate it up.

Her pageboy haircut tucked behind her ears, Tawny Moore asked if Mickey had any regrets.

"Yeah, I always regretted we never got around to looking up my old history teacher, Miss Bainbridge. Now there's a big bad bitch not good for herself or nobody." He delivered the line with a smile, as if waiting for the laughtrack to kick in.

Chuck Watson, of WGN News, asked, "Mallory, if you had it to do again, would you do anything differently?"

"I'd kill the jury, and I'd kill you, and I'd kill you—I'd kill every one of you!"

"What's your favorite pasttime, Mickey?"

"You mean aside from what I'm being tried for?" The crowd's bodies pressed up against the serial killer despite the best efforts of police. Several reporters managed to laugh. Mickey Knox was a pretty funny guy. "I'd say watching TV."

In unison they asked, "What's your favorite show?"

"*Have Gun Will Travel*."

Doing an end run around the crowd, Wayne managed to get in the last question as well.

"Mickey Knox. Do you have anything to say to the American people?"

Mickey stopped and looked dead into the camera.

"You ain't seen nothing yet."

Testimony that day began with Grace Mulberry's tearful retelling of the "house raid" that left her brother and six of her best friends dead. She spoke in careful, measured sentences, describing her best friend Pam's charity work at the local hospital, the pride she felt when her brother, Tim, was accepted by Princeton for the fall.

Wanda Bisbing directed her testimony with kind words and gentle smiles. This had all been rehearsed over the last two weeks; Grace had used her dead brother's thesaurus to find synonyms for "ordinary" as she described her pre-Knox life:

". . . days were pretty *uneventful* . . ."

". . . the *regular, boring* Saturday night . . ."

". . . in *typical* Tim fashion, he said . . ."

". . . your *average* ranch house . . ."

". . . *common* dead bolt, nothing special . . ."

While describing the noise that brought her to the window that night, "the loudest, ugliest car I think I ever saw," her gaze slipped over to Mickey Knox, who sat slouched in his chair, watching her through wire-rimmed glasses. With his printed silk tie and cheap suit, he looked like an ad for Chess King, a K Mart Mickey Rourke.

Mickey kept watching her, smiling a little as she delivered her testimony. As if unconnected to the rest of his body, his right hand turned a pencil over and over, bouncing the eraser off the table. The sharp point tapped softly, continuously, in the quiet courtroom, like the faucet dripping in a sleeping house. It was enough to break her concentration.

"It was a convertible. A Ford, maybe," said Grace. "I told my brother—Tim—that, um, there was someone, people out front I didn't recognize and um, had he invited somebody else? Because I knew they weren't from around here, not looking like that they weren't."

She started twisting the varsity football ring around her finger. It was Tim's. She'd managed to remove it from his body before the coroners had taken it away. It was all she had left of him, that and the memory of his life and untimely death.

Mickey Knox must have noticed this. He sat forward in his chair, never breaking eye contact, trying to unnerve her.

But Grace would not be deterred. "Mr. Knox—Mickey—came up the front walk, past the junipers, whistling something. Then he pressed the doorbell—"

Bisbing stepped into Grace's line of sight, blocking Mickey. Grace suddenly looked up, as if snapping out of a daydream. She craned her neck for a moment, trying to look around Bisbing, but the D.A. held a finger forward to guide her gaze gently back to the jury box.

Sitting beside her husband at the defense table, Mallory Knox looked up only when she heard her name mentioned, a brief but to-the-point description of cheerleader Angie Childress's death at the mercy of a vacuum cleaner. The rest of the time, Mallory contented herself with doodling on a yellow legal pad. Later taken as evidence, the drawings showed not only latent artistic talent, but also tremendous versatility.

Detective Jack Scagnetti sat in the third row, jumpy and restless. His gaze kept drifting over to Mallory, his eyes riding up and down her slender frame as he watched her draw, her long arms flounced over the table, her lips just inches from the paper. His testimony was not scheduled for the third day of the trial. Sitting around on public display, playing all-American supercop, was making him restless.

Jack Scagnetti needed a smoke and a pee.

Melvin DeForest was struggling with a jammed toilet paper dispenser in the last of a long row of Cook County Courthouse toilet stalls when he heard the door open and someone enter, whistling.

The songbird was Jack Scagnetti, who found himself with his pick of a dozen just-scrubbed urinals. While nature took its course, he lit himself a Kool, despite the presence of numerous signs prohibiting such activity.

The door opened again. This time, "It was a man of maybe about forty, balding but otherwise average in just about every way," recalled DeForest.

"You're Jack Scagnetti, aren't you?" the newcomer asked the supercop.

Jack zipped up and puffed out his chest. "I am. I bet you read my books, right?"

"Never have," said the stranger. "But I've seen your picture on TV. You were there when Mickey and Mallory were caught."

"I was the one who fucking caught them," said Scagnetti, who walked over to the sinks and doused his cigarette in the running water. "Maybe you didn't see that on your little TV."

The man joined Scagnetti at the sinks, washing his hands in silence.

"You can ask anyone here, I caught them," Scagnetti said. Fumbling, he shook another cigarette from the pack and popped it between his lips. He felt through his pockets for his matches, but he couldn't find them anywhere.

"Do you recognize me?" asked the man, standing perfectly still. "A lot of people don't know me without my American Express card."

"The restaurant," said Scagnetti. "You were there at the restaurant in Gallup when . . ."

"Exactly," said the man. "We were both there. We both saw it. I call it the Watchtower. You're the only other person I know who's seen it."

"Who the fuck are you? And why are you here?"

"My name's Owen, Jack. Owen Traft." He smiled. "I'm a concerned citizen."

Suddenly a cry came up from the courtroom. "It was so loud you could hear it all the way through the wall," recalled DeForest.

"What the fuck . . ." said Scagnetti, who turned to open the restroom door and look outside into the hallway.

"What do you suppose that was?" said Scagnetti, turning back to the little man. But there was no response.

DeForest walked out to see Scagnetti looking into all the open stalls, puzzled. "Did you see a little guy . . . ?" said Scagnetti, stopping himself as if the question made no sense.

"Is there another exit to this shitter, other than the front door?" he wanted to know.

"No, sir, just the front door," said DeForest.

Scagnetti wiped his brow, as if trying to massage some reality into it.

"There was this little creep—he was just here," said Scagnetti.

"He looked like he was coming up on a bad case of the shakes," said DeForest. "And then I realized why. I looked around for the little guy, and he was nowhere. It was like he just disappeared."

Scagnetti shrugged a helpless shrug, the kind that all human beings do when standing before a mystery that will never be solved. Then he walked out the door.

Back to the courtroom. Where Mickey Knox was about to go on.

CHAPTER

11

The roar Scagnetti heard from the courtroom was the one that went up from the gallery when Judge Bert Steinsma, the sixty-five-year-old senior justice on the court circuit, had uttered the words "Your witness, Mr. Knox."

Mickey Knox swung a leg over the back of the chair as he stood up, a motion not unlike dismounting a horse. He continued the theme as he straightened his belt and kicked the toe of his cowboy boot into the floor.

"Give 'em hell, baby," cooed Mallory. Mickey tipped an invisible ten-gallon hat to her, and smoothed the brim. She laughed. A few onlookers laughed, too, and Mickey smiled for them. This was all for show.

Steinsma lifted his gavel, but did not strike it. "Mr. Knox, do you wish to cross-examine?"

"I do indeed, sir."

Mickey looked over at the court reporter, sitting idle at her machine.

"Does she have to type everything I say?" Mickey asked. Her typing was his answer. He smiled, turning back to Mallory, who had resumed her drawing.

"Ancay ouyay eakspay igpay atinlay." The typist tried, but her fingers got twisted up.

"Mr. Knox!" roared Steinsma.

"That's Navaho for 'I'm a cunt.' "

Mallory laughed, not looking up. Mickey checked the stands for fans; they were loaded with them.

"Begin your cross-examination now or I will hold you in contempt of court."

Mickey suddenly straightened up, squaring his shoulders. "Yes, sir, I apologize."

Breathing on his hands, touching his hair, Mickey slipped into his best Arnie Becker: a winning smile and a grave seriousness. He approached the witness stand slowly. When he spoke, it was deliberately, squelching most of the trailer-park twang.

"That's one helluva story, Miss Mullbery," he said.

"Maybe to you."

"Grace . . . I hope you don't mind if I call you Grace," he said. She looked up at him, into his eyes, recalling something. He had said exactly those words to her before, reading her name off the equestrian trophies on the mantelpiece. She was tied up on the carpet, the nylon fibers biting into her bare legs, as he spoke to her while slicing the throat of her childhood friend Pam Ripley.

"Grace?" he asked.

She lapsed back out of the memory. "Um . . . yes?"

"I'd like to ask you about the murder of your brother, Tim, if you feel up to it. Did you get along, Miss Mulberry?"

"More or less," said Grace.

"More or less . . . what do you mean by that?"

"Well, he's my older brother," said Grace, finding her balance as she found the courage within herself to look Mickey in the eye and answer his questions. "When we were growing up, there were times we could have very well done without each other. But when it counted, we were close."

"I'd like to talk about Tim's martial arts abilities," said Mickey. "How long had he been studying?"

"He started when he was in the seventh grade, so that would make it nine years," she said, unsure as to exactly what this was leading to.

"And what was the color of Tim's belt?"

"The style of fighting that Tim studied didn't believe in belts."

At the prosecution table, Wanda Bisbing was watching carefully. They hadn't practiced any questions about Tim's martial arts—this was the first Bisbing had heard of it.

As if hearing the prosecutor's thoughts, Mickey turned right to her.

"No belts, is that a fact? Well, then, Grace,

could you tell us what form of martial arts it was that your brother, Tim, studied?''

"He learned several styles, but his favorite was Jeet Kune Do.''

"Jeet Kune Do . . . Now I did some research on that form of fighting, and I found out that Jeet Kune Do was a style developed by Bruce Lee. Did you know that?''

"Yes, that's why Tim studied it. Because it was Bruce Lee's fighting style.''

Pacing across the courtroom, Mickey stopped beside the court reporter, who stumbled at the end of Grace's statement, nervous to have him standing so close. He leaned down to her ear, whispering, "It's okay, I still love you.''

"Mr. Knox, do not speak to her,'' said Steinsma.

He did anyway. "Mallory's always been my Barbarella, but you could be our lesbian queen.''

Steinsma struck his gavel three times. Mickey turned on his heel and looked dead at Grace, the questions continuing as if there had been no interruption.

"Now, I think it would be safe to say that anybody who studied the fighting style that Bruce Lee developed—arguably the greatest fighter in the history of martial arts—anybody who studied that for nine years, that would be a fella who could defend himself. Would you describe Tim that way, Grace?''

"Yes, I would,'' she said.

"Point of fact, weren't Tim's hands and feet

considered weapons like guns or knives? Am I correct on that point?"

"Yes, you are," admitted Grace.

"Yet in your testimony just now, you described that Tim kicked me four times in the head," Mickey said, slapping his hand against his own head in demonstration. "And yet his trained Bruce Lee kicks had little or no effect."

Grace didn't answer.

"Then, after shrugging off four blows to the head like I was Superman, I lifted Tim nine-years-of-Jeet-Kune-Do Mulberry off the ground and threw him across the room."

She still didn't answer, partly because it wasn't a question, and partly because everything he said was true. There was no conceivable way someone could have done that to Tim, yet Mickey Knox had.

He walked slowly to the evidence table, floating a hand over various pieces of evidence. While everyone in the courtroom gasped, Mickey Knox picked up a knife.

The bloody knife he'd used to kill Tim Mulberry.

"Then I took this knife . . ."

Mickey was walking toward Grace, putting his finger on the sharp point in a painful pantomime. "I took this knife and proceeded to tear your brother limb from limb. And your brother, whose hands are lethal weapons—"

"Objection," shouted Bisbing, jumping up, incredulous that Steinsma was letting this happen.

"Defense is intimidating the witness with the murder weapon."

"Had little to no defense . . ." continued Mickey, moving closer and closer.

"Sustained," said Steinsma, suddenly waking up to the danger that was present in his courtroom. "Mr. Knox, put the knife down."

Grace was not going to be intimidated. "I don't know how you did it, but you did it!"

"Mr. Knox! The knife!" shouted Steinsma, motioning for the bailiff, who signaled the guards.

Mickey stopped moving and sniffed the knife. "Still smells a little like Timmy," he said before returning it to the table. He retrieved his pencil.

"Now, Grace, how do you think a human being could possibly be capable of doing something like that?" asked Mickey.

"I don't know!" she yelled, surprising even herself.

"Now . . . I don't believe that, Grace," said Mickey, who seemed to be peering into some corner of her psyche that only he could see. "I think you have a definite opinion on how I was able to do those things you described. Now, I'm going to ask you again. And I want you to remember you were under oath."

Standing in front of the witness box now, Mickey Knox brought all the force of his personality to bear on poor, young Grace. He began once again the slow, rhythmic *tap-tap-tap* of the pencil rubber, bouncing it off the mahogany witness box just to unnerve her.

"In your opinion, Miss Mulberry, how was I able to murder your brother, Tim Mulberry, in the manner described?"

Grace, who had returned to twisting her brother's ring, looked up into Mickey's eyes. There was a certain stillness in her heart.

"You're not human." Her lips curled funny when she said it, but she was dead serious. She had held it together for her entire testimony, but now she was starting to cry. "I thought about it a lot. And the only thing I could figure is you're not human. . . . I don't know if you're a vampire, or the devil, or a monster, or a cyborg, but you're definitely not human!"

"Thank you, Grace," said Mickey, who seemed so satisfied with her answer that he probably couldn't have written a better one himself. "I have just one further question."

"What?" asked Grace, relieved to be almost done with the entire proceeding.

"Do you believe in fate?" asked Mickey.

"What?" asked Grace, clearly confused.

"Do you believe you have a choice about when it's your time to go?"

Wanda Bisbing had had just about enough. "Objection, Your Honor. What does this have to do with Grace Mulberry?"

"You want to know what this has to do with Grace Mulberry, Miss Objection?" Mickey said, turning to Bisbing. "I'll tell you what this has to do with Grace Mulberry. It's her time!"

Faster than anyone in the courtroom could

even comprehend what was happening, Mickey Knox plunged the pencil in his hand deep into Grace Mulberry's chest. Over and over he stapped her, blood gushing out as he plunged the sharp lead point into her aorta, her lungs, her very heart.

"Show off!" shouted Mallory gleefully, gathering up her drawings.

Jack Scagnetti saw his opening as the courtroom erupted into pandemonium and everyone rushed to save a girl he knew was already dead. "How are you doing, Mallory?" he asked, pulling out a cigarette.

"Well, it's not Paris."

The bailiff and two security officers pounced on Mickey, pulling him off as he broke off the pencil inside Grace's body. He landed the stub in a guard's leg. It wasn't a full-out fight, because he knew there was no point.

The cowboys had all the bullets.

"No further questions, Your Honor!"

CHAPTER
12

Dear Mallory,

First of all, I want you to know that you are my all-time hero. Ever since I first heard about you on TV, I knew that I had to meet you. I guess because this is a letter, it's really not the same thing as meeting you, but I feel like I already know you, so this is just sort of to introduce you to me, like you care. If I were as cool and famous as you, I probably wouldn't care either.

Even by comparison to my friends, whose lives all pretty much suck, mine is much, much worse. I know you think I'm exaggerating, but I'm not. You have to believe me, because why would I lie to you? Boys hate me and my teachers think I'm stupid. Even my cat doesn't like me anymore. Don't laugh, it's really true. It's like it smells a dog on me, but I haven't been around any dogs at all. I've become this horrible hate-me monster and you're the only person I can think of to help me.

I need your advice about killing my parents. I know

you're way too cool to try to talk me out of it (like I said, I think we're like sisters or something, it's weird), but I do want you to know that they really are unbearable and it's not like it's going to get any better tomorrow, so none of this wait-and-see stuff, okay? Cool.

I guess I should tell you a little bit more about my situation so you'll see exactly why I have to do it, and maybe offer me some tips on how to do it (creatively!) without getting caught. I know you got caught, which sucks, but it's super-romantic that you're in jail with Mickey, who fought for you and all. I don't have a boyfriend at the moment, so there's no real incentive to get caught.

Which I guess is my first question, sort of out of order, but hey. Should I get a boyfriend first? If so, who? Obviously, you don't know who's available, so let me give you the rundown. (Sort of like a lineup!)

RANDY—is in my first period English class, and he's really smart. He doesn't act so smart in class, which makes sense, because if he did, they would take him out of the class and make him go to the honors classes, which are really hard. But I know that he's really smart because he'll say the smartest things out in the hallway or during lunch. Things I never thought of, about death and infinity and stuff. On the plus side: He's smart, like Mickey, and he's into death, which is (duh) very important if we're going to start killing people. Minuses: He's probably more talk than walk, and my dad could kick his ass if it came down to a fist fight. (But we would use guns anyway.)

MANNIE—I'm including just because he's my best, best friend on Earth, but he's not really boyfriend material because he reads my Cosmopolitans and watches Power Rangers just for the Tyrannosaurus Rex guy. (He's cute, though!)

GARRETT—I hate, but he's a good choice for a couple of reasons. First, he already drives, even though he's not old enough to (he parks the car a few blocks away from school—smart!) and second, he already has a gun. I'm not sure what kind it is (what do you recommend?) but I know that he can use it, because I've heard other guys talk about how he shot cans with it a few weekends ago, and hit every one. Pluses: drives, has a gun, good aim, probably would be willing to kill my parents. Minuses: asshole, not clean, listens to Poison. (Yes, *still!*)

Should I team up with Garret, or Randy, or just go solo? Tell me if this is too weird, but I was also thinking about partnering up with one of my girl friends. That way we could both kill our parents and drive off like *Thelma and Louise*. Did you see that? I liked that a lot. A must-rent. When I think about you and Mickey in the desert, it looks just like that movie but with Mickey driving instead of Susan Sarandon. My friend Tisch and me, we could do it. She took judo after this guy attacked her mom last year, so she's tough as shit.

Thank you in advance for your advice. I have to go—I'm writing this in sixth period health class (my advice: don't get shot!) and it's just about over. So hey, take care. I hope you guys break out soon! Come stay with me!

Love,

Sara Wu
Newhall, California

Dear Mallory Knox,

You don't know me, and you didn't know my sister, either. But that didn't stop you from killing her. She was one of the four people you shot in the Dair-E Freeze in Genoa, Colorado on July 15th of last year. She was thirteen years old.

Do you even remember Genoa? It's a tiny town a few miles off the interstate, just this side of the Kansas border. Like most people, you probably pulled off to get gas, having assumed there would be other towns, when there weren't. The thing is most people, they fill their tanks, then they leave. They don't start shooting people.

I'm writing this letter so you can know exactly who it is that you killed. With all the bodies stacking up everywhere, the faces must blur together for you. I am not going to let that happen. If you're even capable of having nightmares, I want you to play this over again and again in your mind. I want you to go to Hell with this picture in your head.

Katie McCaslin was the blonde in the back corner by the windows, sitting with her friend Lisa (brown hair, chunky) sharing a plate of fries. According to Earl, the cashier you left alive to spread the legend (why?), you asked for a Diet Coke in a place that only

serves Pepsi. For that, four people died. According to
Earl, Katie was the last one you shot. *You* shot her,
not your boyfriend/husband/whatever the fuck he is.
You pointed the gun and you killed her.

What was going through your mind when you pulled
the trigger? Did she remind you of someone, something, sometime? I just want to know who fucked up
your wiring so bad that you thought a thirteen-year-
old girl made a good target.

I'm sure you're the product of a broken home,
parents who loved too much, or not at all, or fingered
your ass when they gave you a bath. I don't care.
Everyone goes through horrible shit, but that doesn't
make it right for them to become serial killers.

Mallory Knox, if you ever leave that prison, I will
hunt you down and kill you. Death probably doesn't
scare you that much, but I will make you pray for it. I
swear to God I will see you in Hell for what you did.

Eugene MacCaslin
Genoa, Colorado

Dear MALLERY KNOX,

Lifetime incarceration can make a person feel that
the Lord has abandoned him, that Christ his Son died
only for other people's sins and couldn't possibly
have love in his heart for Murderers, Rapists and
other Criminals.

Yet through the miracle of Salvation, you MAL-
LERY KNOX can know the glory of the Light, and
feel your soul unburdened from the shackles of Evil
and Distrust that placed you in this captive state. Even

as you spend the rest of your natural life in prison, you have been given the gift to ask for God's Grace to spend your Eternal Life in the freedom of His love.

MALLERY KNOX, it is the Holy Bible, the Testament of God's work on Earth that provides the Key to this Redemption. In its glorious pages you will find the Answers to the questions about God's plans for you, humanity, and his Kingdom. With the power of His Word, you can take your place among the choir of his Angels, singing His eternal praises. I implore you to seek solace in His heart. It is large enough to hold the entire world, from Saint to Sinner to you, MALLERY KNOX.

Spreading the news of God's glory,

Jack Alamenenti
The Christian Murderer/Rapist Support Network

Dear Mallory Knox:

I'm writing on behalf of veteran journalist Wayne Gale, the popular and respected anchor of the top-ten television program *American Maniacs,* to request the opportunity to interview you and your husband Mickey for an upcoming episode of our show. This is the third such letter I've sent to both you and Mickey; I am assuming that either (a) your mail is not being forwarded in accordance with prison regulations, or (b) you have received the letter and do not wish to participate in such an interview.

If the former is the case, rest assured that our well-placed government contacts will be alerted to the situation, and watchdog groups such as Amnesty International will be mobilized to protest this injustice.

If the latter is the case, I would like to explain why *American Maniacs* is an ideal forum to express your opinions and viewpoints:

- The show is the highest-rated crime-oriented news program on television today.
- Unlike syndicated shows such as *Hard Copy* and *Inside Edition, American Maniacs* is network-based, which enables us to promote and advertise this specific episode nation-wide.
- Veteran anchor Wayne Gale is one of the most respected interviewers in the business, having interviewed everyone from Charles Manson to David Berkowitz. He will provide an uncensored forum to express your opinions to the American public.

Again, I hope you receive this letter and seriously consider allowing us such an interview. If so, by the law of the state of Illinois, you may contact us through your court-appointed legal representative, who is required to convey your request. It is a felony for anyone, even a member of the penal system, to attempt to prevent this lawful communication.

Sincerely,

Julie Gwenheiler
Producer, *American Maniacs*

cc: Dwight McClusky, Warden

Dear Mallory,
If you could, I'd like you to settle an argument for us. It arose one night after a fair quantity of controlled

substances were consumed and/or inhaled, sparking a heated discussion that ranged from teleology to television.

Do you remember the show *Fantasy Island?* You know, "Duh plane! Duh plane!" Sure you do. It was on after *The Love Boat.* So here's the question:

Was Ricardo Montalban (Mr. Roark) supposed to be God or the Devil?

We felt you would be uniquely qualified to answer.

I argued that there was a part they always edited out of Fantasy Island, where Tatoo would hand out a hit of acid just as each of the guests were getting out of the plane. They tried to disguise it behind all those hula girls who put orange yelllow and pink leias around everyone's neck, but little Tatoo was there giving each person his or her prescribed dosage.

Then, at the end of the final season, I think we were supposed to find out Mr. Roark was evil incarnate, and all those people he had doomed their souls to eternal Hell by succumbing to their desire in this world. But then the network guys figured, hey, why not have a Vegas scene instead, with lots of girls in tight sequin costumes. (Who likes those costumes anyway? I don't think I would want to know anybody who really likes those costumes. Although on you, Mallory, I would make an exception.)

The Mr.-Roark-Is-God contingent argued that each of the encounters was designed as some sort of personal trial, and thus were really just a manifestation of the Joseph Campbell epic-quest model of a personal heaven.

Me, I think my fantasy would be to visit Fantasy

Island. But it wouldn't be very good for the storyline, because I would get off the plane and boom, the fantasy would be over. "That is the fantasy you are living right now," Mr. Roark would say, and then where would I be? I would just have a brief appearance at the beginning and end of the show. Me and Jorge Luis Borges. (Argentine surrealist writer. I'm coming off as a pompous ass, aren't I? I'm sorry. Although it's strange to be apologizing to a woman who killed over 75 people.)

So, Mallory, how did mainstream America buy into the concept of this show, when it is clearly so drug related? Just once I want to see the camera pull back, so we can see the person in the fantasy sequence taking a drag off a monster bong.

Sound good?

Chad Calley
Sophomore, Yale

Dear Mallory,

You are a vile, cruel, despicable creature and we here at Sigma Phi all want to suck your hot pussy. If you get out maybe you can make it to one of our "theme" parties. "Kill the Guinea Pig Night" was very successful—over two hundred people. We strung a big fat guinea pig over the living room by its hind legs and took turns stabbing it with an ice pick and holding a lighter to its face and plunging pencils up its ass while it screeched like a banshee. The object of the game was to keep it alive as long as possible. This one actually went for six and a half hours. I guess that's why they're called guinea pigs. Tish, my girl-friend, really got off on it and tried to stab it so hard that I had to stop her. (She's starting law school in the fall—she reminds me of you). I later took Tish to the couch and fucked her and she said it was the best sex she ever had listening to that ball of fur die. Since that time we've had a "Kill the Pussy Cat Night", "Kill the Puppy Dog Night", and "Kill the Vietnamese Pot Belly Pig Night"—man, did *it* screech! Some chick from the Veterinary school heard about it and she barged in screaming and trying to pull it down so Tish sat on her stomach. We finally tied her up on the buffet table and it looked like things might get out of hand when two football players sort of started to rape her, but believe it or not she actually began to like it. She ended up riding that sandwich like a pro and got cummed on at both ends while Brent, who's pre-med, cut out the the pig's eyes. (Yes, it was still alive! I wonder where its pig mother is—or if she cares). We had another problem which we turned to our advan-tage when Inez, our housekeeper, threatened to go to the Dean. We told her we'd turn her in to Immigration and that shut her up. To teach her a lesson we threw a surprise "Torture the Housekeeper Party". *No,* we didn't kill her—but after we got her pretty scared we all took turns pissing on her. (She quit the next day). Later while fucking, Tish she told me how much she wanted to kill her—she said it would be the ultimate screw. Never having killed anyone I wouldn't know. I sometimes think I'd like to, but getting caught is too much of a hassle. I've got one more year of undergrad and three years of business school ahead of me and I

don't want to jeopardize any long-term commitments.
I've heard of places in Thailand where you can buy
someone to kill (usually some schmuck or schmuckess
who needs to provide for their family) and that would
probably be fun. Maybe Tish and me can go there on
our honeymoon? She always says that violence is the
true spirit of Mother Nature. The Marquis de Sade
said cruelty is perfectly natural. I suppose that makes
us all ecologists. And you and Mickey are our pagan
gods. If Tish and I weren't so into getting our degrees
and making money we'd do what you did. Kill some
for us!

Josh G.
Stanford University
Palo Alto, California

Ms. Mallory Knox:
 On behalf the InterPacific Product Company,
Lmtd., we are authorized to offer $15,000 to Mallory
for using Likeness and Body of Mallory Knox on
children toys including:

 (1) Mallory Knox plush doll "squeezable", 30 centimeter

 (2) Mallory Knox "Born To Die" lunch box and
Thermos

 (3) Mallory Knox hair comb "switch-blade"

 (4) Mallory Knox girl bike stickers

Please advise.

Galen Eng
(fax number listed)

Dear Mallory,

I was reading in *Spin* about how they won't even let you have pencils, so I want you to know its okay that you haven't written back. You would if you could.

Just wanted to let you know that I started going out with Garrett (the guy with the gun) and he's a lot cooler than I ever would have guessed. In fact, he's a total teddy-bear deep down. He puts up this asshole front to keep people from getting close to him, because he is afraid that if someone gets to close they'll hurt him. *Sassy* did a story on it a few months back that completely makes sense looking at it now.

So in a funny way, my life's going a lot better than the last time we talked. I'm sure it's that psychic bond between us, your advice coming through even if you don't realize it. Garrett was definitely the right choice.

So anyway, I'll let you know when we kill my parents. I'm getting to be a pretty good shot, so I don't think it will be too much longer.

Life is so cool.

Sara Wu
Newhall, CA

Mallory—

You don't know me yet, but I was sent to help you.

At first I thought it was the other way around, because you and Mickey were the ones that helped me see through the fog to the Watchtower. Yet now I realize that this was part of a deeper plan all along. It's hard to imagine just how far the web reaches, or how strong the threads are, pulling us together.

Trust me that when the time comes, I will be there.

—Owen

More than 1,100 letters addressed to Mallory Knox were discovered in warden Dwight McClusky's office following his death, unopened and unread. During her stay at Stateville Prison, Mallory officially received only four pieces of mail: two magazines, two bills.

CHAPTER
13

For the wasted lives and bartered souls that were marking time at Batongaville, it was the incessant drone of gangsta rap that dictated the mood of the place. More regular than a heartbeat, it reached into the viscera and pulled your poor helpless volition into alignment with the sweaty fear and vulgar rage that shook the building to its foundation. It was the soundtrack to an atmosphere steeped in boredom, straining under the burden of the endless, oppressive hours and minutes and seconds that strung together to finally mark the passing of another day. The music gave voice to a dark reality of the human spirit that polite society had isolated behind walls of barbed wire and lines of armed guards in a pathetic attempt to deny power to its own most primitive impulses.

There was no escape at Batongaville.

Twenty-two-year-old prison guard Shawn Devlin wore a cross around his neck. He was frequently ambivalent about his faith in God as he roamed the halls of the prison, but was unwilling to take the chance that he might be wrong and commit himself to a fiery eternity in hell (which he couldn't imagine to be much worse than doing a stretch of time in this place). But the pay was good, the hours reasonable, and for a guy who was six-foot-four, two hundred and twenty pounds, and willing to play ball, the work was fairly nondemanding. Still, the assignment they gave him to escort that famous TV guy, Wayne Gale (who, as he arrived at the prison, took it over like he was moving into a new condo or something), was about the strangest thing Shawn had ever been asked to do.

A huge convoy of semis arrived at five that morning, though the interview wasn't scheduled to take place 'till after the Superbowl that evening. Shawn had money on Buffalo, even though he knew Dallas would probably win; that was how much he hated the Cowboys. He wished he'd been able to kick back that Sunday night with his buddies, down a couple of beers, and yell at the Bills for being a bunch of pussies and losing the game in the first quarter like they probably would. Still, he thought, watching this irritating little pest talk to Mickey Knox on live TV would give him something with which to talk up women in bars for years. He had no idea when he pulled the assignment quite how big the story would be.

As he escorted the crew through the central

corridor on their way to the visitation area, where
Wayne would have his "showdown," as he was
now referring to it, with Mickey Knox, Shawn
was handed a note by Wayne's producer, Julie,
whom he had managed to discern didn't have a
tongue. She was given to scrawling notes with
maddeningly bad penmanship and handing them
to him when she wanted to know something.

"Is it dangerous for women here?" she wanted
to know.

Shawn thought for a moment of Helen O'Hal-
loran, a woman he'd known from the Joliet Baptist Church, who was drawn to Batongaville in
the grips of an ecstatic vision. The Holy Spirit
had sent her on a mission of redemption to save
the souls of the Lord's most abject sinners. But
what Helen found at Batongaville one solemn
Sunday afternoon in a corridor off of B-wing was
more reminiscent of visions of the Apocalypse.
Isolated for a moment, she was brutally gang
raped by the very sinners she had come to witness to.

What Shawn really thought was that God would
turn his back even on angels in Batongaville. But
he didn't want to frighten the woman. "No more
dangerous than it is for anybody else," he said.

The place smelled like hell right now, but that
was common whenever the "cons" as Devlin
called them (at least in polite company) went
nuts. (They, in turn, referred to the guards as
the "police," making no distinction between any
asshole in a uniform.) Recently, they'd beaten up

a couple of guards, so Warden McClusky had had the prison on lock-down, and there was nobody to empty the trash. With no ventilation, the place was always hot and steamy even in the winter time, and the stuff just sat there, mildewing in the halls. The cons were out now, and the trash had been removed in anticipation of the camera crews arriving, but the stench remained. As they walked the halls, the cons either eyed the crew suspiciously, or came up talkin' shit. Devlin wished they'd keep 'em locked down all the time—they were a whole lot less trouble when they were in their cells. He'd long since grown deaf to the slick stories they were so adept at spinning. It was only the poor do-gooder from the outside who got an earful of why this one was unjustly imprisoned or why that one was denied due process. Sometimes Shawn wondered why this prison was full of black men being guarded by whites, and how he'd feel if the situation were reversed, but mostly he didn't like to think about it.

"Tell me. You can tell me—Shane, is it?" said Wayne.

"Devlin. Just Devlin."

"Right. Tell me, Devlin. Has Mickey Knox's arrival here affected the attitude of the inmate population? You know, killing other guards and prisoners and all. From the working man's point of view."

Devlin just shrugged and said no, not really. But if he'd been honest, if he'd felt like Wayne was someone he could trust, he would've said that he'd been spooked since the day Mickey had arrived. The whole place was up in arms. You could feel it in the air—sometimes it was hot, like a wave of anxiety and fatigue that hits you just before the fear sets in, and sometimes it was cold, like icy fingers on your spine. Everyone stops talking, starts listening, because it could come at any moment and from any direction. And the silence only made the place more creepy. Silence is a dangerous thing in prison life; it's the calm before the storm.

And the arrival of all this hoopla was guaranteed to make things worse. Devlin didn't know why McClusky let this guy and his crew take over the prison when it was such a hotbed already. He didn't know why the warden let the caravan of equipment and media people pull up in front of the place and disgorge their contents into the prison, stirring things up when they were already bad. His dad was retired now from the Corrections Department, but his Uncle Vernon was still on staff at Batongaville; Vernon liked to say that no matter how bad things got, it was never anything compared to the riot of '75. He told Shawn not to worry, that soon the Knoxes would be gone, and the place would get back to normal. But Shawn hadn't asked him. And Vernon had coincidentally taken the next week and a half to go fishing in Colorado.

"Give it to me straight," said Wayne. "I want to know everything there is to know about *Batongaville*." The word rolled off his tongue with an

almost lecherous delight. Wayne liked the sound
of it so much, he repeated it a few times. *"Batonga, Batonga, Batongaville.* Tell me about the
place. Give me the . . . the . . ." He looked to
Julie for help, who signed back to him without
missing beat. "That's it, Zeitgeist. Give me the
Zeitgeist of the place. I want to know what it's like
to have my freedom taken away, to have my
spirit crushed underneath the cruel wheels of the
American justice system." Wayne went on, lost
in the rhapsody of his own prose, but Shawn
couldn't remember the rest of what he said, since
he was receiving orders on the walkie-talkie from
his C/O at that very moment to hold the crew in
the hallway.

"What are we stopping for?" asked Wayne,
keen with anticipation. "Is something wrong?
Something you're hiding from us? Something
we're not supposed to see?"

No, Shawn explained, the prisoners from P/C
were going into the dining room, and nobody else
was allowed to come in contact with them.

Julie whipped out a pen and began scribbling
madly, but Wayne was faster.

"P/C? What's that? Are they political prisoners? Sequestered? Is the administration trying to
deny them their right to talk to the press?" Wayne
wondered anxiously. He could see this dovetail-
ing brilliantly with the intro he was planning to
the interview.

"No," said Shawn, "P/C means protective
custody. It's mostly the snitches who'd be killed

if they came into contact with the general population, and the old guys who just don't want to mix it up with the gang bangers who run the cell blocks.''

"You mean they're segregated in there because they want to be?" said Wayne, incredulous. "Fascinating. You have to tell me much, much more," he said, but not really waiting for a reply as they walked into the giant, five-tiered B-Wing.

It was the longest of the corridor-style prisons in the country, and a pretty nasty place to be; the older, more hardened guys lived there. They didn't have as many violent outbursts as the roundhouse, which was full of angry young punks, but when they got mean, somebody usually wound up dead.

"What did he do? And him? And him?" begged Wayne. "God, I love this. It's just so . . . so . . . *real*."

Shawn gave him the guided tour:

CELL #2543: Raymond Sojack. Age fifty-six, one of the only whites on B-Wing. Convicted in January, 1993, of murdering his wife and two children in suburban Chicago with a knife. An accountant who had never had so much as a parking ticket in his life, his plea of insanity due to excessive economic pressure had been denied by a jury of his peers. Since arriving at Batongaville, Raymond had found God and repented his sins. Time spent doing clerical work for the chaplin conveniently allowed him extra privileges that other prisoners did not enjoy. Devlin was skeptical, but then again it really wasn't his business.

CELL #2544: "Big Al" Forrester. Second in command of the biggest gang in the country. Six feet, six inches tall, he tipped the scale in the medic's office that only went to three hundred pounds and nobody knew by how much. When new inmates appeared in B-wing that "Big Al" took a fancy to, his lieutenant Dave "Mad Dog" Mac-Millan would approach the tender youngster with an invitation—to join Big Al in his cell before lock-down that evening. Advantages to going: He'd dope you up with so much "medication," you'd probably never feel a thing. Disadvantages to not going: Major bones would be broken. Big Al favored large and painful fractures, usually hip bones. Mad Dog's advice to Big Al's inamorata: "Smell nice and wear something frilly."

CELL #2544: "Slim" Acosta. Sixteen years old, but didn't look a day over twelve. Convicted for shooting and killing another teenager to get his jacket, he had arrived at Batongaville without any gang associations strong enough to prevent him from becoming a catamite for "Big Al," or anyone else who wanted him, for that matter. "The kind of guy you find one day swinging from the ceiling on a sheet," said Devlin.

CELL #2556: Devlin referred to this inmate as "Chester the Molester." It was the first and last time he ever asked an inmate what he'd done to get in here. "It makes my job a lot easier if I just don't know," he said.

CELL #2558: Owen Traft. Sure didn't look like the type you'd usually find in Batongaville. Much too ordinary. Devlin remembered that as Wayne walked by, Owen stood up and grabbed the bars of his cell, and shouted after him—"You're Wayne Gale! I guess this isn't as real as TV, is it, Mr. Gale?" Devlin thought it was a joke or something, but if it was, the guy didn't seem to get it—his comment was delivered without a trace of irony. It vaguely gave him the creeps.

But Wayne didn't hear a thing as he traveled blithely on down the hallway, as he was on the phone just then, a cellular that they'd ordinarily confiscate from him at the gate. They weren't really allowed inside the facility, but the guards at the salley port whose job it was to clear all the equipment had had their hands full at the moment Wayne arrived. Movie producer Don Murphy was pitching a full-blown Hollywood fit just then, demanding to see Mickey Knox before they severed his hemispheres and he was no longer competent to sign over the rights to dramatize his life. Wayne resented Murphy's status as the best pitchman/biggest bastard in Hollywood, and normally would have taken him on for invading his turf, but that could wait 'till the next time he spotted him over oysters-on-the-half-shell at Babylon. He decided to count his blessings and silently thanked Murphy for allowing him the opportunity to sneak through with the cellular.

As Wayne traveled through B-Wing with Owen Traft at his back, Devlin recalled that Wayne was too consumed in a conversation with his girlfriend, Ming, to notice. She didn't seem to be too happy about Wayne's latest gift, and wanted to exchange it. "Exchange it? It's a Tiffany bracelet, not an airline ticket," shouted an agitated Wayne.

If he hadn't been so busy on the phone, Wayne might have realized that the prisoner who was now following after him in the hallway in a dazed stupor was none other than *the* Owen Traft, who had delivered ratings gold to his biggest competitor, Oprah Winfrey. The incident had sent Wayne into a headlong dive into a bottle of Prozac for a month, and it probably would have pissed him off beyond belief if he'd ever realized who Owen was. But Wayne was not the most self-aware guy who ever drew breath, and probably never realized it was no coincidence that they were all here at Batongaville together.

The topic for the day had been "Women who Love Too Much," an old standby that functioned as a catchall for guests and specialists who couldn't carry a show by themselves. Theme music blaring, Oprah had arrived on stage, the camera panning across a wave of admiring fans clapping for the sheer joy of the noise, the sound of the ocean sucked back through rocks. Like most days, the applause lasted about twelve seconds before the hostess launched into her first question: "Women, have you ever wondered if you're loving your man *too* much? Today we're going to talk to three women who put their men on a *love* diet, and find out from an expert how to tell if you're treating your man nicer than he *deserves*. You with me on this, women?"

The women in the audience cheered, some housewives in sweatshirts shaking their arms above their heads like lazy cheerleaders. The APPLAUSE sign continued to flash. "I can tell it's ladies' show today. Am I right?" Oprah turned dead-on to camera. "Girlfriends out there, pull your chair up close, because we got a lot to get talkin' about."

After four shouting matches, three tearful confessions and two commercial breaks, Oprah opened the floor up for questions. Owen recognized the first two women, having seen them on the show at least three times before. They had a lot of poise for amateurs, he thought.

Owen kept his hands raised throughout the questioning session, but Oprah kept picking women who stood up or waved their hands frantically, wanting to answer back to something a guest just said.

Then, faintly at first, he began to hear it: a pulsing sound so deep it barely registered, like a timpani in a distant auditorium. As it came closer, the edges of the sound became audible, the scratch of a broom on cement just before and after the pulse, louder now. There was a top note, too. An echo, the shadow of the sound. Rubbing his eyes, he looked forward, seeing the source more clearly than he ever had before.

A globe of light hung in the center of the stage, floating unaffected in the empty space. The pulse came from the blinding glare of the searchlight beam as it spun past, rotating three-hundred-and-sixty silent degrees. Owen checked around him, but no one else seemed to notice it there, the happy idiots blind to the Watchtower before them.

Just as Oprah was turning, Owen raised his hand. She caught him out of the corner of her eye, and stepped back to him. As he stood up, she raised a hand, motioning him to wait a moment for the speaker to finish. Inches away from her, he could smell her perfume and hairspray. While the audience began booing the man's brutish reply, she put the microphone in his face, nodding for him to start. A shot of adrenalin suddenly kicked in.

"Uh-uh-I had a k-k-k-question."

"Go ahead."

As he stared at the spinning light, time seemed to expand. The extra seconds gave him the opportunity to see himself in the monitor, the studio light shining through his thinning hair. He had plenty of time to reach into his jacket pocket and find the proper grip. He had time to articulate clearly.

"I just wanted to know," he said, "is death painful?"

From his pocket he pulled the small silver gun with its small silver bullets. He raised it at full arm's-length. Took aim at the couple farthest on the left. And fired.

It was just like remote control. But louder. One by one the panelists slumped backward or forward in their chairs, each hit once in the chest or head. For a man who had never fired a gun in his life, Owen's aim was astonishingly fatal. Inhuman, as one investigator would later describe it.

Like a stone dropped in the audience, a ripple formed as the crowd tried to get away from him— mothers and daughters crawling over each other and tucking themselves into the aisles. They needn't have worried. Once Owen had fired all four shots, he tried to hand the gun—still smoking—to Oprah, who had dropped to the ground and was scooting her way up the steps.

While the crowd and crew bolted for the doors, Owen sat calmly in his chair, waiting for the police. He wouldn't put up any resistance as they shoved his face into the carpet and cuffed his wrists behind him, the rings so tight they cut off his circulation. They could punch him, kick him, spit in his face, but he would deny nothing, and do his best to appear perfectly sane as he confessed his guilt.

Justice was served swiftly, and within a month Owen Traft was just where he wanted to be—

doing time at Batongaville. Home of Mickey Knox. And now, things were even better, if that was possible, for Mallory Knox was here, at least for the evening, until she and Mickey were to be shipped the next day to Nystrom Asylum—"Lobotomy Bay." As he watched Wayne Gale disappear down the hallway, he was certain that all of the elements were converging for him here at Batongaville. Something had entered in through the front gates with Wayne and his trucks, and you could feel it all over the prison. That silent, ineffable disquiet, an electrical current of anxiety that was radiating throughout the halls. He didn't know what exactly fate had in mind for him when he'd heard the voices tell him to quit his job and drive across country to purchase that gun in Chicago, but they hadn't led him wrong yet. He could hear them hollering in his brain even now, but what they were saying wasn't yet clear.

Whatever it was, it was coming soon.

CHAPTER
14

At the same time Wayne Gayle's crew was converging on Batongaville, Katherine Ginness's plane was touching down in Albuquerque, New Mexico.

In the twelve months since their capture, Katherine Ginniss had read just about every word written about Mickey and Mallory Knox, ostensibly as research for the profiles at Quantico. It was part of her fixation on "statistical wholeness" argued Dan, an orthopedic surgeon she dated on and off. To a degree, his diagnosis was correct. She was the kind of person who spraymounted jigsaw puzzles once finished, locking them in place for eternity.

Yet truth be told, she wasn't convinced that all the pieces to the Mickey and Mallory puzzle had been found, much less fit together. While the overarching reality of the case was inescapable—the Knoxes had killed at least fifty people—there seemed to be gaps that everyone else was willing to overlook, unlikely conclusions forced into slots where they didn't fit. With a Ph.D. in criminal psychology, she wasn't a woman given to hunches. But something felt wrong.

She rented a car in Albuquerque, and was on the road to Gallup before the sun had worked its way into shining. It was Sunday, an unusual day to meet on official business with the Gallup County coroner, but she was on her own time on this one. Not to mention her own nickel. She arrived at the coroner's home just as the sky broke into bright, blue New Mexico daylight.

Earl Johnson had served with distinction as coroner and medical examiner for Gallup, functioning mostly as a one-man show, except for the occasional three-car pileup or nursing home fire. When she had called from Washington to set up the meeting, he had seemed reluctant. In person, he seemed openly hostile.

"I hope you don't mind if I tape record this," she said, as the machine came to life. "It's standard procedure for us."

"No, that's fine," he replied.

GINNISS: Testing, one-two. Katherine Ginniss interviewing medical examiner Earl Johnson at his home in Gallup, New Mexico. two-thirty P.M.

JOHNSON: I use one of those. Sony?

GINNISS: Panasonic. For autopsies, I'll bet.

JOHNSON: That, and I'm writing a book.

GINNISS: Not about Mickey and Mallory, I hope.

JOHNSON: It's fiction. It's about this medical examiner

in a small town who solves murders that no one else figures out.

GINNISS: Like that show, *Quincy*.

JOHNSON: Not really. Here, this should be the one you need.

GINNISS: Is this your only file on Hailey Robbins?

JOHNSON: It's the only one you need.

GINNISS: That's not my question.

JOHNSON: That's not my problem.

GINNISS: Will I get to see other files?

JOHNSON: Everything you need is right there.

GINNISS: I guess that answers my question.

JOHNSON: I'm sure you'll think of others.

GINNISS: Mr. Johnson—Dr. Johnson—I don't want you to think you're under investigation here, because you're not. I am here only because we noticed some inconsistencies between the Hailey Robbins death and the others attributed to Mickey and Mallory Knox.

JOHNSON: Such as?

GINNISS: Such as why she was killed when other hostages were set free, if in fact she ever was a hostage. None of the other victims were strangled. None of the other victims were moved after their death. Also, we can't seem to fit her death into the chronology of events as we know them. I'm not accusing you of any wrongdoing. I just hoped you could answer some of these questions.

JOHNSON: Let me address your charges one at a time, if it please the court. First, the young woman was clearly held captive in a manner similar to each of the three other Mickey and Mallory victims. The details are nearly identical.

GINNISS: Except that the three other hostages are alive. Hailey Robbins is dead.

JOHNSON: Ms. Ginniss, I'll leave it to your department to determine *why* they killed her. I simply deal in concrete facts, *how* she was killed. She was strangled. The evidence of that is unassailable.

GINNISS: Our killers typically used a gun or a knife.

JOHNSON: They also used fire on occasion, and a fish tanks and a Heineken, if I'm not mistaken. Strangulation isn't such a leap of faith when you think about it in those terms.

GINNISS: Like Mickey and Mallory's other hostages, you believe that Hailey Robbins was bound at some point before she was killed.

JOHNSON: That's correct.

GINNISS: Yet your reports don't give any indication of wounds to the wrists or ankles, anything to indicate she was tied up. No fibers, no burns, nothing. If she was bound, she would have struggled against the ropes, probably to the point she began bleeding and it became too painful. That's pathology 101, Doctor.

JOHNSON: If you're suggesting I overlooked something that significant, you're welcome to take a look at the photos. Look through this file. You'll find her wrists and ankles free of contusion. But simply because there are no rope burns does not mean that she wasn't bound. There are many ways she could have been restrained. Duct tape, for instance—

GINNISS: Would have left residue on the skin, which you

apparently didn't test for. Also, it would have ripped out the hair on her wrists when it was removed. And why would Mickey or Mallory Knox bother to remove the tape anyway? Taking the time to tidy up the body would indicate a refraction period, a moment of ritualization. I don't know if you've examined the other forty-nine coroners' reports, but they weren't exactly known for being tidy.

JOHNSON: All right, Miss Ginniss, I would like to know why you are here. I would like to know why you find it necessary to resurrect this tragedy, revisiting pain and suffering not only on my staff, but also on the Robbins family, who have spent this last year trying to lay their daughter to rest.

GINNISS: Dr. Johnson . . .

JOHNSON: You come in here with your badge and your bitchy attitude and tell me that I handled this examination incorrectly, when in fact I am the only one in this room qualified to discuss matters of forensic pathology. You have no business here, and no invitation. I have, sitting on the desk in my office, the business card of one Inspector Clark—your superior if I am not mistaken—and will not hesitate to call him if you do not stop these questions immediately.

GINNISS: Dr. Johnson, I'm looking at a write-up in the file you just handed me, and it says here that skin tissue was removed from under three fingernails on her left hand. Probably from clawing her attacker in a defensive move.

JOHNSON: Very common in these cases.

GINNISS: It wasn't in the report.

JOHNSON: I'm sure you're mistaken.

GINNISS: It would also tend to dispel the theory that she was tied up. Kind of hard to scratch somebody with your hands tied behind you.

JOHNSON: I'm certain I don't see your point. If you'll excuse me, I am going to call Inspector Clark.

GINNISS: It says here the tissue was type O-negative. Yet Mickey and Mallory were both A-positive, were they not? Who did she scratch, Dr. Johnson? Her killer? If so, the one thing we know for certain is that it wasn't Mickey or Mallory Knox.

JOHNSON: There's another explanation for that. If you'd just shut up for two seconds so I could think. . . .

GINNISS: You knew there was a mismatch, that's why you left it out of the report. You deliberately withheld evidence in a federal case. Besides being a felony, it's a hell of a way to lose your examiner's license.

JOHNSON: It was an oversight. That's all it was. I noticed it about a month after we filed the paperwork.

GINNISS: You had the opportunity to go back and correct the file. That happens all the time in federal cases.

JOHNSON: This is not Washington, Miss Ginniss. It's Gallup. And believe it or not, things like this don't happen every day out here. Most of the time, I'm just here to say, 'Yup, that was a suicide,' or 'No, the driver wasn't drunk.' What these people did, it was the most horrifying thing I'd ever seen. The Asian fellow who Mickey shot up in Drug Zone, that was the most arduous cleanup you could ever believe. I mean, pieces of his skull were embedded in the wall.

GINNISS: I believe you.

JOHNSON: So then I notice that the blood types don't match and I ask myself who really benefits by digging around more. This girl Hailey Robbins is dead and buried, no matter what I say, and is it really worth dragging her family through this again? They believe, as I still believe, that Mickey and Mallory Knox killed their daughter. I can't place them at the scene of the crime, but in my heart of hearts I know it's the truth. I'm afraid I just don't see the use in stirring up a dead fire.

GINNISS: Because whoever killed Hailey Robbins has gone unpunished.

JOHNSON: You just want the glory. Admit it.

GINNISS: Doctor, there's still a killer out there somewhere.

JOHNSON: After twenty years, trust me, there's killers everywhere.

Katherine Ginniss called her secretary at home, interrupting his church barbecue and asking him to track down Jack Scagnetti ASAP. He called back within minutes, informing her that Scagnetti was already at Batongaville in anticipation of escorting the Knoxes to Nystrom the next morning.

She estimated she could get back to Albuquerque by eleven A.M.; an eleven-forty flight would put her in Chicago at three, and allowing for traffic, she could be at Batongaville by five. She told her secretary to book the flight.

Everything was starting to come together.

Jack Scagnetti was wandering the halls of Batongaville Penitentiary, trying to remember just how many murderers he had sent here over the years. At least a dozen, he decided, although the faces blurred together.

But nobody like Mallory Knox. Nobody *ever* like Mallory Knox. He remembered how she had felt in his arms as he had carried her the night of her arrest, ostensibly the responsible police officer just doing his job, but secretly cradling her more preciously than Salome caressing the head of John the Baptist. And now he was on his way to see her once again.

It was halftime, the game threatening to become a blowout, with the score stretching to 20–3. But most of the prison seemed to be consumed with watching the Bills getting their asses kicked, leaving Scagnetti to reacquaint himself with Mallory Knox without much interference.

This was why he'd taken the job. Not, as that idiot McClusky had wanted, for the purposes of blowing Mickey Knox's brains out in a no-contest fight while the poor bastard was handcuffed to the bars of some prison bus in the middle of the Mojave. But to see Mallory again.

He wondered how much trouble he'd get off the two thick-necked cowboys who were there to "protect" him, as if he needed protection.

"I can smell her," he said as they were still two floors away. "Can't you? It's the same smell I got off her sheets in Vegas." He was starting to sweat. His feet echoed as they hit the linoleum— was it giving way to her singing? Was that the sound taking shape in the distance?

"I think that's your beeper, Mr. Scagnetti," said one of the guards.

He didn't recognize the number as he dialed it in the sergeant's office, but the clicks and static told him it was probably a car phone. A woman's voice answered.

"Detective Scagnetti? This is Katherine Ginniss."

The FBI chick. The last person he expected, or wanted to hear from. "Kathy, what's hanging?" He wondered if she'd get the subtle implication that he meant her ass.

If she did, she wasn't interested in sparring. "First, I need to tell you that this call is being recorded, Detective."

"What, are you my broker now, Kathy? Or my bookie?"

"Federal laws say I have to disclose that."

"You feds, you're always on top of things, aren't you?"

"I want to ask you a few questions about one of the Gallup murders."

"Shit, Mickey and Mallory? That's a while back, Detective." He pulled open one of the desk drawers, found a stack of *Playboy* inside. "Oh,

I'm sorry, are you a detective? I don't remember what they called you.''

"They call me Dr. Ginniss, not Kathy, and I'm an FBI investigator.''

"That's right. Now what can I help you with, Doctor?'' The static was building up on the line, with Ginniss evidently approaching the edge of a cellular network. Scagnetti hoped to himself that she might lose her connection. But a second thought plagued him. Where was she driving that she was almost out of cellular range? Nowhere on the East Coast, certainly.

"I'd like to know what you could tell me about Haily Robbins.''

"I honestly don't remember that name. Was she a victim?''

"Her body was found in a dumpster at a drive-in theater. Evidently, she was a prostitute who most people knew as Pinky.''

Scagnetti reached forward and quietly pushed the door closed. "And you say this was in Gallup?''

"Yes. We know you were at the crime scene.''

"How is that?''

"You signed the police report which attributed the murder to Mickey and Mallory Knox.''

Sitting back in his chair, he reached for a cigarette out of the crumpled pack in his pocket. "Now, I'm starting to remember this. It was one of their last murders. At least, one of their last murders outside of prison walls!'' He tried to

punch this last part into a joke, but couldn't even
hold his own smile.

Before Ginniss could ask another question,
Scagnetti started in: "I can't see why any of
this would interest you, Doctor, considering both
Mickey and Mallory signed a statement in which
they confessed to killing this woman."

"Along with forty-nine other people."

"Exactly. That's why they're serial killers."

"Earlier this week I spoke with the prosecutors
who drew up that confession statement, and
learned that Mickey and Mallory weren't ques-
tioned about each individual killing. What they
signed was basically a list of names, no locations
or descriptions. There's no way they would know
who most of the people on that list were."

Scagnetti lit his cigarette, setting the still-smok-
ing match on the desk, where it burned a dark halo
on the steel. "Let me help you out, then, Doctor.
I'm actually at the prison right now, getting ready
to chaperone our killers over to the looney hospital
in the morning. I'd be happy to ask one or both of
them about it, just to make sure."

"That won't be necessary Detective. I'm actually on my way there right now."

Scagnetti's throat went dry. His hand with the
cigarette began to twitch a little. "I guess I don't
understand why."

"I'd really rather discuss it when I get there,
Detective. I simply called to let you know I'd
be there soon and ask you to meet me in the
warden's office."

"We'll talk about it now, Doctor, or Kathy, or whatever the fuck you want to call yourself," said Scagnetti, his voice pitched in aggravation. "Are you casting aspersions on my investigative skills?"

Ginniss was silent for a moment. She was usually a polite, matter-of-fact individual, but after all Scagnetti had put her through, all the insults and aggravation and macho obstreperousness she'd had to endure from him, she couldn't help getting in a dig.

"No, Detective. I think they're excellent—when you want them to be. Maybe even too good. It's always amazed me how uncanny your ability was to think like a killer."

No one will ever know what was going through Jack Scagnetti's mind at that moment, but it's clear from the silence on the phone that he knew the game was up. His instincts were far too good not to know that Ginniss was onto him; and that if she was, he was easy to pin down. It wasn't until later, long after events would come to pass and Jack Scagnetti and Katherine Ginniss would no longer care, that results came back from the lab linking the torn tissue under Haily Robbin's fingernails with the marks that appeared on Jack Scagnetti's face on the videotape from the night of the Knoxes' arrest at the Drug Zone.

Ginniss had him nailed. His obsession with killers, born on the day Charles Whitman had climbed to the top of the University of Texas watchtower and begun picking off strangers one by one, kept bleeding over into each and every minute of his life until Scagnetti could no longer resist its temptation. The horrific event that had ripped his mother from his life had a power and a lure that was as seductive as it was repellent; and in the end, he could no longer struggle against its pull. He longed for the thrill, the sexual release reserved only for those he obsessively tracked. And now it was over.

One thing was for sure: There was no way Scagnetti was going on the run. He would have left the prison then and there. Perhaps Ginniss's call was even meant as an opportunity to let him run? Maybe she wanted to add to his humiliation by hunting him down. Or maybe she only wanted to offer him the dignity of a fellow law officer, give him the choice to end it his way. Scagnetti didn't know for sure. But whatever he was thinking, it was clear as he signed off that he had resigned himself to the inevitable.

"Good work, Doctor. A lot of people would have missed something so trivial. But not you."

"Thank you, Detective. I'll take that as a compliment, coming from the best."

Silence.

"So, then," she said, "I'll see you when I get there."

Scagnetti laughed. "Not if I see you first."

He hung up the phone, and stepped out of the office. He was a man who still had an engagement to keep.

With Mallory Knox.

CHAPTER
15

Dwight McClusky was not a happy man.

When he'd agreed to let Wayne Gale and his traveling sideshow into Batongaville to interview Mickey Knox, he had no intention of ever coming through on his promise. He'd merely been humoring the so-called "journalist" into thinking he'd get what he wanted. At the time, Mickey and Mallory were scheduled to be shipped off in three weeks for Nystrom, and the unbelievable bureaucracy involved in getting permission to do anything through the Illinois Department of Corrections made it well-nigh impossible to requisition a paperclip in that amount of time, let alone schedule a live network interview.

How was he to know that prick Gale had the lieutenant governor in his back pocket?

Back in 1975, McClusky's predecessor at Batongaville, Santino Gonzales, was one of the "new breed" of wardens with a master's degree in social work who had written his thesis arguing against capital punishment. One day a scuffle broke out in the lunchroom, and before the day was over, they'd had to recapture the roundhouse from the control of the inmates. Six people lay dead.

Gonzales retired, and now toured the country speaking in support of the death penalty.

It had taken Gonzales almost an hour and a half to get to the prison in rush-hour traffic on the day of the riot, commuting as he did from Chicago to Joliet every day, and two guards were dead before he ever showed his face at the prison. The Corrections Board had therefore established the requirement that his replacement reside in Joliet, which made the job a lot less attractive, since few of the top dogs in the corrections business wanted to raise their families in a rural prison town.

But Dwight McClusky had openly campaigned for the job. He may not have been the most brilliant and qualified of applicants, but he liked the idea of ruling with an iron fist over one of the toughest max joints in the country. He had no kids to think about, having lost Dwight, Jr., in 'Nam in '68, and Bryon now worked for the Alpo corporation in Cincinnati, Ohio. His wife of forty-four years, Maxine, ran a knick-knack shop in Joliet proper. She didn't mind life in a prison town, so long as she didn't have to hear about it every night when Dwight got home.

But McClusky was just about stretched as tight as a drum as he watched this bunch of "jackass media types" (as he fondly referred to them) trying to take over his prison. The kind that petitioned the courts for permission to watch federal executions take place, then puked all over themselves at the spectacle. They'd built the observation room in Batongaville on a slant for just that purpose, for easy washing down after the event was over.

McClusky looked on in disgust at the exhibition before him. Shawn Devlin, who was positioned by the gate with gun in hand should things get out of control, had never seen the warden look so worried before. He was flanked as usual by his two sidekicks Kavanaugh and Wurlitzer, a cloying, sadistic pair who fawned over his every word. Devlin later recalled that McClusky had been nervously fingering the nose pliers attached to his belt, which he favored as a means of prisoner intimidation as he watched the sound guys, camera people, production assistants, makeup girl, and other "essential personnel" (as the network application had termed them) turn his prison into a sideshow. Potted plants, zebra-skin rugs, and leather armchairs had been just the beginning of what to his mind was becoming a ridiculous fiasco. McClusky watched Gale with a burning hatred as the Superbowl played in the background.

It was near the end of the fourth quarter, and the game that had threatened to be a blowout had, at the two-minute warning, narrowed to a margin of 20–17. Panicked network programmers were on the phone with Wayne, warning him that the interview might be delayed if the game went into overtime. Wayne's high-pitched shriek was barely decipherable at that point, but Devlin noted that it contained something about calling his father-in-law.

If Wayne Gale was a mess, Mickey Knox was as cool as a Zen master in contemplation of some inner landscape. He had shaved his head for the interview, and his sit-com good looks, contrasting with his homemade tattoos made him seem even creepier than he had before. McClusky and Wayne seemed to be vaguely unaware of his presence in the room, but Devlin was sure that despite his apparent detachment, not a detail went by that Mickey Knox was not aware of.

When he had been led into the room ten minutes before, a panicked gasp had gone through the crew at the sight of his bald head, fresh white skin stretched tightly over his large skull, eyes bigger and darker than ever. Scotty was the first to recover from the shock, quickly readjusting the lights to eliminate the anticipated glare off the killer's head.

"It's a pleasure to see you again, Mickey," said Wayne, holding out his hand to shake, but Mickey was still chained tight, cuffs to belt to legs. Mickey didn't say anything, just glared strangely, looking from under his upper eyelids as he surveyed the room, a tiger in a new cage.

"Could we get you some makeup for your head, there?" Wayne asked, still trying to be chipper. Julie and the rest of the crew had backed away, unconsciously. Mickey smiled and shook his head.

As the guards led Mickey to his chair, Wayne could see his career disintegrating before his eyes. Whatever they had done to him in prison had burned out some circuit in Mickey's brain. Gone was his sense of humor, flair, individuality—everything that made him a "Manson for the '90's." Now he was just another Gacy, deathly dull.

Suddenly, Wayne looked around, as if seeing the room for the first time.

"There were twelve of us guards with the Mossberg twelve-gauges positioned around the perimeter," said Devlin. "It's hard to imagine he simply hadn't noticed us before." But Wayne flipped like an interior decorator who's suddenly discovered the walls of his Frank Lloyd Wright house have been covered with Nagels.

"Oh, my God," he screamed, pulling McClusky into intimate hearing zone. "Dwight—you don't mind if I call you Dwight, do you? Dwight, could I have a small word with you?"

McClusky was suspicious, but nervously assented. Wayne put his hand on McClusky's shoulder and walked him around the room.

"You met the kids I have working for me?" Wayne said.

"Yes, I did."

"Great bunch, aren't they?"

"Seem to be . . ."

Wayne didn't wait for a complete answer.

"Scott, genius cameraman. Roger, magician with sound. Josh over there, as fine a playback operator as you'll find anywhere. Herb and Frank, my lighting guys, couldn't do without them. Maria, my assistant, indispensable. And Julie, my producer, well—I could sooner do without my arm than Unruly Julie."

"Is that her real name?"

"Just a little nickname," said Wayne. "Yep, they're my kids and they're all I need. After working together these past coupla years, we're like well-oiled machinery. No, more like a formula race car. No, scratch that one, too. What we're really like is a Swiss watch. Small, intricate, compact . . . it shouldn't work as well as it does, but it does. Because of the craftsmanship, the expertise, and the artist's loving hand."

Wayne gave McClusky a moment to digest this. It wasn't going down well.

"Now, Dwight, I don't know if you've ever been on a set before--"

Dwight puffed up at this. "Ya know, I was."

"Really?" asked Wayne, with feigned enthusiasm.

Devlin watched the amusement pass over the faces of the crew, who had obviously seen this before, but McClusky had the biggest ego in the state of Illinois and Wayne's flattery was clearly influencing him.

"I was on the *Dukes of Hazard* set about eight years ago."

"Well . . . small world," said Wayne. "Then,

you know firsthand how Hollywood does things. Lights all over the place, generators, a hundred and fifty crew members . . ."

"Oh, that *Dukes of Hazard* show, there was probably ninety-five people there, maybe more. Not to mention the General Lee—that Dodge Charger—they had at least three, four of them. Guess they didn't drive away from them crashes as clean as they did on the show—"

"Right," said Wayne, interrupting what was promising to be one of McClusky's tireless diatribes on his encounter with Tom Wopat. "Anyway, you see what I mean. It's a funny business, isn't it?"

"It sure is."

"They got an asshole over here," said Wayne, pointing to his left. "An asshole sitting down reading a magazine over there. An asshole perched up there. Assholes everywhere. Hey, maybe if we were doing that kiss, kiss, bang, bang stuff we'd need all those assholes, too. What we're about is intimacy. We're about two people having a conversation. Say I was interviewing you. All I want you to worry about is what I ask you. I want a trust to develop. If you're thinking about all this," said Wayne, waving his arm as if to reveal the room for the first time, "you're not going to relax, a trust won't develop. We'll be talking at each other instead of to each other, there will be no chance for intimacy."

Wayne gave McClusky a moment to take all this in. Devlin had to give it to Wayne—he was good. He'd found McClusky's weak spot, and he was pushing it hard.

"Which brings me to what I want to talk to you about." He escorted McClusky to the opposite side of the room from where Mickey was sitting, so as not to let Mickey hear what he was saying, talking to McClusky in a whisper. "I have to get Mickey Knox to relax . . . Mickey Knox to relate . . . Mickey Knox to share what he's never shared before . . . Mickey Knox to answer what 'till now has remained unanswered. Mickey Knox to open doors which 'till today have been closed. Well, how can we expect him to do that when we've got Department of Corrections guards up the ass?"

McClusky suddenly tripped to what Wayne was driving at, pulling away like a jackrabbit. "Well, just what the hell do you expect me to do?"

"Lose 'em."

"Mr. Gale, do you have the slightest idea how dangerous Knox is?"

"Warden McClusky, I assure you, I am very familiar with Mickey Knox's career."

Now the gloves were off. Out-and-out anger filled the air.

"Since he and his wife have been in custody, they've killed . . ."

"Don't recite the facts to me, Warden. I'm sure I know 'em better than you do."

"Well, let me in on one fact you obviously don't know. If I were to take my men away, Mickey Knox would snap your neck like a twig."

Wayne was hot now, twisting his words in an

Australian frenzy. "One, I can take care of myself. I grew up in a tough neighborhood, and I've handled some pretty rough customers in my day. Mickey Knox does not scare me. Two, I'm a journalist, and I'm prepared to take that risk. Three, it ain't gonna happen. Believe me when I tell you, mate, it is in Mickey Knox's best interest to play this game according to Hoyle."

Wayne must've realized what the rest of the room had toppled to long before, which was that McClusky was not someone you could bully, and at this moment he was holding all the cards. Wayne shifted gears.

"Wait a minute," he said. "We've gotten into an adversarial relationship here, which is not what I want. But seriously, Dwight, look at this." Wayne scanned the room, counting guards. "We've got one . . . two . . . three . . . four . . . seven . . . twelve . . . guys. I mean, Jesus Christ, Dwight, that's too much. Let's lose some of these guys."

"Wayne, if it was anybody else—"

"Dwight, I'm just scared he's gonna clam up on me with all these sherries all over the place. Their shotguns poised, ready to blow him in half if he scratches his nose. Possibly me as well. They hate him. He hates them. What kinda intimacy am I gonna create with all this hate in the air? Even you and I feel it."

"What are we talking about?" said McClusky. "Two guys?"

"Okay, I'll take two guys off."

"No, no, no, no, no, no, I mean only two guys."

"I can't do that. Seven guys."

"Three."

"I'll cut it in half. Six guys, but that's it."

Wayne smiled gleefully over the victory as the final buzzer sounded, signaling Shawn Devlin's loss of thirty bucks as the Buffalos went down to Dallas, 20–17. He wasn't upset about the money at just that moment; he was more worried about the six of his buddies that McClusky was sending out of the room, wishing he was going with them. But there was nothing he could do.

And that was how Mickey Knox came to be watched by only six guards as the cameras began to roll.

Quietly, almost inaudibly and seemingly to himself, Devlin heard Wayne whisper:

"Showtime. . ."

CHAPTER

16

Dearest Mallory,

You once told me I had no feelings. You were right and you were wrong. I got more feelings now than I ever had before. I never missed someone like I missed you. My cell is so cold. At night I get the chills. I pretend you're lying next to me, holding me from behind with your leg draped over mine and your arms wrapped tightly around me. I lie in my cell and imagine kissing you. Not making love, just kissing for hours on end. I remember everything about our time. I remember every joke you ever told. I remember every secret you ever shared. Shared or revealed? I think shared is proper.

I remember every single time you laughed. I remember every meal we ever ate. I remember your cooking. I remember watching *David Letterman*. I remember driving fast behind the wheel of the Dodge Challenger, and you, baby, by my side. Your bare feet up on the dash, singing along with the radio to your favorite, Patsy Kline, and your dancing, my God, your dancing, on the hood of the car to "Sweet Jane" while the angels flew by overhead. I never told you before, 'cause I didn't want to disturb them by calling your attention to them, for fear they'd fly away. But from the first moment I saw you, Mal, you were surrounded by a halo of light, and I could see them, swimming and swirling around you, and I knew that you were my salvation.

Sometimes it's hard to talk about all the things that are inside of me. That's why I got so pissed off at all them dumb psychiatrists and stuff who want to psychoanalyze me and chop up my personality like you could lay it out on a table and say well this part here is the killing part and this part here is the loving part and this part here is because his daddy yanked his dick and this part here's because he didn't get no shiny new bike for his sixth birthday like he was fixin' on. That one guy Dr. Reingold, he ain't psychoanalyzing anyone any more is he? I guess you showed him didn't you baby, that's my girl. But you know every time I took a shot and the bullet hit the mark, every time I threw that knife and it landed true, the nature of the universe would reveal itself to me, and I could feel that precise moment of crystal clarity, where I knew, I just *knew,* baby, that it's all the same thing. There ain't no parts. It's just an illusion. I am everyone and everything that ever lived. It's what some people call God. And you're the mirror that showed it to me, baby. You and your angels. You're teaching me something I never knew before. You're teaching me how to love.

All God's creatures know it's painful to grow, but I am indeed growing. I know you were pretty pissed off with me right before we got caught, on account of me killing the Indian and all, and oh I guess that hostage business too a little bit, but we can discuss that later. Anyway, killing that Indian was an accident. But sometimes you gotta pay your karmic debt for accidents too, 'cause it was karma that caused you to commit them in the first place. There ain't no innocents, no way, baby. Not even you. But our time of delivery is at hand, I can feel it. That part of me that just knows these things, when other people don't—well, I guess I just got done saying how there ain't no parts and all, but I guess the other side of being the whole thing is containing its separateness, too—that part is telling me that our time is near. When our existence will change shape and we'll no longer be locked in this puny world of delusion and pain, but we'll expand and be released into a whole other level of existence. I can feel it, Mal. The pain is so acute. My skin is sensitive even to the touch of sunlight, the smell of rain on the wind hurts me to breathe, it's like the pain of birth all over again, but I'm being born into a world that mere human beings can't even imagine. And you'll be with me, baby, by my side. That is why in this time of transformation I inspire myself with thoughts of our time together. I go through it hour by hour. I don't jump ahead either. I take it as it comes, and I live that day again. The way we were when we first kissed . . .

(Unfinished letter found in Mickey Knox's cell after the Batongaville riots, January 30, by Illinois state police. Mysteriously disappeared, and was auctioned off by Christie's Auction house in July of that year for $25,000.)

CHAPTER
17

At the time of this writing, there is probably no one in America who hasn't seen the infamous Mickey Knox/Wayne Gale interview broadcast live from Batongaville after the Superbowl. It shook America into a new awareness of just how sick and depraved its own fascination with shock media had become. Like a traffic accident on the freeway, it drew the public's eye inexorably even as they tried to look away.

At exactly 7:42 P.M. Central time, immediately following the victory of the Dallas Cowboys over the Buffalo Bills, the network promo for the interview hit the screen of the television in the B-Wing rec room, accompanied by a picture of Mickey Knox.

"And now, Wayne Gale goes one-to-one with Mickey Knox. Straight from Batongaville Penitentiary—on the eve of Mickey Knox's lobotomy. Is he or isn't he? Let America be the judge. . . ."

"It was like a razor went slicing through the air," recalled "Mad Dog" MacMillan, who at the time was watching the show in the B-Wing rec room. "Cut everybody. Nobody was gonna get up and go about their business once they saw Mickey Knox's face on the TV screen. The man that had been makin' the joint jumpy from the day he got there a year ago, and everybody in the country was watchin' that motherfucker now. Talkin' 'bout how the wolf don't know he's a wolf, the deer don't know he's a deer, God just made it that way.

"I don't remember exactly when it was, but I think it was when he started talkin' that demon shit—yeah, I think that was it—sayin' something about the demon living inside you, how everyone's got the demon. Feeding on their hate. Cuts, rapes, kills, uses your weakness, your fear, about how only the vicious survive.

"Well, man, if you want to see hate and fear, and you come to Batongaville, you come to the right place. Minute he said that, it's like something went off. But somehow, right then, didn't nobody need a reason. I look over and see that kid, Slim, who's always got kind of a crazy look to his eyes anyway. He's looking up at the TV screen, and whatever Mickey Knox is talkin' about, well, Slim, he sees it too.

"Next thing I know, there's a garbage can flying through the air. Smack into the middle of the TV set. It explodes like fireworks on the Fourth of July. Something like that happens, the police—they're a bit jumpy anyway—they got guns up on the catwalks, walking up and down the cell block, they start firing warning shots into the air. Whatever that crazy motherfucker was puttin' into the air or the drinking water, I don't know, but everybody just seemed to go bust at the same time.

"The next thing I know, everybody is mixing it up. There's police in the rec room being beat to death with chairs and table legs. The police up on the catwalks are firing like crazy as they climb up and over the razor wire, it's like these motherfuckers don't even feel it as their skin's being cut to ribbons. They fire and fire and fire. And they still keep coming.

"Somebody starts dragging mattresses out of the cells and setting them on fire. Don't know what they was thinking, 'cos big as this place is, them mattresses are made of foam rubber not feathers, and this smell like burning plastic fills the air and can't nobody breathe. By that time, the police turned off the water, so nobody can put it out and we start breaking the pipes out of the walls and ceilings just so we won't choke to death.

"If a place ever looked like hell, I'm telling you, man, this was it. The power goes out, so the only thing lighting the place is the fires. Water is coming down from the ceiling and steam's filling the cell block. I'm looking down at my feet, and there's three inches of water already, and its running red, man, I tell you no lie. Motherfuckers throwing paper and police and whatever they got over the railing. I look up and I says to myself, David, my man, you better bend over and kiss you sweet ass good-bye, because this is only the beginning.''

It was at the end of the second commercial break, right after Mickey Knox had confessed to Wayne that he thought of himself as a "natural-born killer," and Shawn Devlin saw McClusky on the phone. "Whatever he was hearing on the other end of the line, he looked like he was about ready to pop a hemorrhoid."

"Where? For the love of Pete! . . . Okay . . . Okay . . . Mobilize the men. I'm on my way." McClusky hung up the phone and took his last clean breath. *"Close down all the cameras!"* he screamed.

"Is this a joke?" cried a disbelieving Wayne. "Are we finished! We're live for chrissake. We got another ten minutes! Two hundred million Americans are—"

"We got a riot going on in the rec room in B-Wing. They got guns, hostages, explosives. Close it down *now!*" said McClusky, with a finality that nobody at Batongaville had argued with in nineteen years.

But Wayne Gale was not a man easily defeated. "Then could we go with you and film it? Dwight, for chrissake! Live!"

"You stay here and you shut up!" said Mc-Clusky, who was about two inches away from putting Wayne out of his misery for good. "I got to see what the hell's going on down there before I can let you film anywhere. It all *started* 'cause of your goddamn show in the first place."

Wayne followed him out of the room. Trying to grab him. Desperate. "But the world is watching, Dwight. You can never get 'em back! You'll be famous. It's history! Dwight!"

Wayne's outrageous set of balls managed to push McClusky past violence and into incredulity. He turned to Kavanaugh. "This asshole's still tryin' to tell me what I'm gonna do in my jail. Fuck him! This nanderfuck don't know what he's dealing with here, but we do. And he ain't gonna be responsible, we are. So keep your shotguns, your fingers on the triggers, and be ready to fire at a moment's notice!"

Recalls Shawn Devlin: "Somehow at the time, I knew that heading out into the middle of a riot with the warden was no place I wanted to be, and that staying in that interview room was probably safer, but I gotta tell you, when he called for me to go with him I was glad to be going. I remember as I was going out, looking over at Duncan Homolka, who was eating like his tenth donut of the day, and thinking Lord, thank you for getting me the hell out of this room, because I don't want to be anywhere near that cracker Mickey Knox anymore."

As the gate closed, Devlin took one last look at the four guards left behind with Kavanaugh. His friends and drinking buddies.

Within the hour, they would all be dead.

* * *

As Jack Scagnetti approached Mallory's cell with two guards in tow, he had no idea what was happening in B-Wing. Even if someone had told him, he was beyond comprehension. He had entered a tunnel there was no escape from and he had no choice but to follow it to its end. At the end of the tunnel stood Mallory Knox. Singing to him, drawing him closer, like a siren calling Aenaeus to jump to the sea and into the arms of death.

"I told him he shouldn't go in there alone," said Frank Lesh, the guard who was with Scagnetti on that fateful trip. "I think he thought he could handle her. A lot of guys had made that mistake before, and hadn't lived to regret it. But what can you do? The guy's like a federal supercop or something. The warden says to do what he wants. I'm thinking, hell, maybe he's tougher than me, but I sure as shit wouldn't want to be in there alone with her."

"Rise and shine, Knox," said Scagnetti as he knocked on the door. Lesh opened it for him, Scagnetti walked in, and told them to leave. "I looked at Austin, the guy I was with, and we thought about it for a second, but neither one of us particularly wanted to cross him, so we left."

"We went back into the hallway, and neither of us was trying to listen, but we could hear them murmuring and her laughing. She has a scary, psycho-bitch laugh that you only hear in your dreams. Nightmares, more like it. It's like a dirty sex laugh. And I think, well, maybe there's something between a super cop and a super killer, maybe he's gonna get some in there after all. Me, I'd rather stick my dick in ground glass. But Austin and me, we figure what we don't know we won't be blamed for if the shit hits the fan, so we walk off down the hall to have a smoke.

"The next thing you know, Scagnetti's screaming like a stuck pig. I go running for the door, but Austin has the keys, and we're both so fuckin' freaked watching this eighty-five pound chick about to snap this big guy's spine, we can't hardly get the door open. We pull her off and Scagnetti, he's so pissed he whips out his gun and I swear he was gonna shoot her right there if we hadn't started yelling for him to stop. You'da thought she'd just told him he had the tiniest dick in the world or something, because for a minute there he just could *not* let her live anymore in this world. But then he took a breath, and then another, and then finally I took one 'cause I knew he wasn't gonna shoot her.

"He grabs Austin's mace and starts spraying her. And at first I'm relieved, because he didn't shoot her, but then he's spraying her and spraying her and spraying her and she's screaming and screaming and she may be a killer and all but she's a woman, too, and it's getting hard to look at. I was thinking about trying to stop him but suddenly all hell broke loose and the next thing I know, I look over and Mickey Knox is at the door carrying a shotgun. Before I can even think,

Austin goes down and the world is in slow motion and I get off a shot just as I feel the heat of a shotgun blast throwing me back against the wall."

"It's the last thing I remember."

After Dwight McClusky had left the interview room, Mickey Knox decided he was a comedian.

Guards who worked on his cell block in isolation recall that he used to stand in front of the mirror all the time, telling jokes he'd read in his Playboy joke book over and over again. He never got tired of hearing himself tell them, and he was his own best audience. Some of them were even funny.

So he was in good form when he started to tell the joke about Little Johnny going to the drive-in with his big sister and her boyfriend, Bobby.

"He was circling the room, like he wanted each and every person to get his joke," recalls Herb Gaines, a member of the *American Maniacs* crew. "At the time, I thought, wow, the guy really needs to be the center of attention. But afterwards, when I thought about it, I remember he was looking closely at everyone. Seeing which guard was alert, which one was caught up in the joke and wouldn't be so quick to fire. It was brilliant, really. And I still don't know how he did it. I don't know who's looking out for me that I didn't get shot in all that gunfire in a room that was no bigger than fifteen by fifteen, but I'd like to take the opportunity to thank whoever it is."

The official joke, from the Playboy guide, goes something like this:

So the mother says to the sister, "Okay, you can go to the drive-in movie with Bobby as long as you take Little Johnny." The sister says okay. They go to the drive-in, and they come back. The mother gets Little Johnny and says, "Okay, what happened? Where did ya go?" Johnny, who can't talk, acts like he's kissing. "They kissed," said the mother, "what else?" Little Johnny squeezes imaginary breasts. "He felt her up, what else?" Little Johnny starts undressing. "They took off their clothes, what else?" Little Johnny panto-mimes a fucking motion. "They did *that*! What were you *doing*?" Little Johnny vigorously jacks off.

"Everyone in the room is laughing at this point," recalls Gaines, "including Mickey himself, who's holding a donut he picked up from the Winchell's box on the way over to stand near Kavanaugh. As he threw the donut to Homolka, who was a surefire bet to catch it, Mickey adds the capper to his joke, yelling 'Little Johnny, no!'"

"I guess he figured out pretty fast that Kavanaugh was the most alert, the best shot in the room," said Devlin later. "Maybe he just figured that as the warden's pet, he had the most to lose."

In a flash, Homolka's attention was on catching the donut. Mickey grabbed Kavanaugh's rifle and shot across the room, hitting Zendel first and then Powell. In what could only be described afterward by investigators as a lucky break, when Powell went down, his gun went off, hitting Kurth—a big, friendly guy who was known for being a little slow—and killing him as he went down.

"You'll never get out of here, Knox, you're dreaming," said Kavanaugh, lying on the floor in a state of shock after all the gunfire had cleared and it was apparent to everyone in the room that somehow, Mickey Knox had held the day. To punctuate the victory, Mickey bent over and snapped the trigger finger on Kavanaugh's right hand.

"I am the most dangerous man in the world, Kavanaugh." He snapped the trigger finger on Kavanaugh's left hand. Kavanaugh let out an ear-piercing caterwaul. "And when the most dangerous man in the world tells you to do something, you oughta think twice before refusing."

It was clear Kavanaugh was not going to give Mickey Knox any more trouble. Nor was anyone else. Mickey instructed what was left of the crew at that point—which comprised Roger Brinks, the cameraman, Herb Gaines, the sound guy, Josh Richmond, the playback operator, and Julie Gwenhirly, the producer—to follow him. Wayne Gale was discovered cowering underneath the desk.

Instructing Roger to get an image on the portable betacam or lose his life, Mickey then signaled the hostages together out the door. Homolka and Kavanaugh followed, hands in the air. Everyone else was dead.

"You take me to Mallory's cell, Kavanaugh," said Mickey. "And you better pray she's in one piece."

As the door opened, Wayne had a last-minute afterthought to grab the cellular phone off the desk. And as a result, America became witness to the most bold, outrageous prison escape in the history of the world.

Antonia Chavez's place in journalistic history was assured in a classic case of being in the right place at the right time.

Having started out as an entertainment reporter doing puff pieces on celebrities and the occasional society bash, she had taken over the second-banana spot on the ten o'clock news at the third-ranking Chicago station two months before when management decided to overhaul the format of their flagging show. Indeed, her propensity for see-through blouses had actually jacked the ratings up in recent weeks.

When the call had come through from the network that they were establishing a live feed from Batongaville, where Wayne Gale and his crew were in the middle of a full-scale riot, producer Scott Mabbutt looked down at Antonia, who was being prepped for the ten o'clock promo spot by hair and makeup people. She's not ready for this, he thought. But none other than the head of the network, Wayne Gale's father-in-law, had called the station manager with the dictate that they begin broadcasting live. Right then.

The guys in standards and practices were going nuts. It was impossible, they said, to broadcast live—there was no way they could control the flood of images that came across the airwaves and into the homes of America. An entire generation of children could be damaged by what they saw paraded before them. But the network had seen the opportunity to leap into an undisputed first place for the season which would lock in top-dollar advertising rates for the next. It was thus decided that the broadcast would go out on a sixty-second delay, the network taking the position that almost anything it showed would be defensible in the pursuit of journalistic authenticity. The result was that whoever wound up with their hand on the edit button didn't exercise it very much that night.

A title card filled the TV screens across America:

"SPECIAL REPORT"

The network announcer's canned voice sent chills down the collective American spine. "We interrupt this program to bring you a Special Report."

Antonia Chavez was shoved in front of the camera, wrestling to fit her earphone into her ear.

"Good evening, I'm Antonia Chavez and this is a WDN Special Report."

The live feed was patched into the station, and Scott Mabbutt gave a low whistle at the spectacle that appeared before his eyes on the screen. Never, anywhere in the history of broadcast news, had he seen anything like this. He began speaking into Antonia's ear in as calm and reassuring a voice as he could manage. "We're taking you right now live to Batongaville Penitentiary . . ."

"I'm being told that we're taking you right now live to Batongaville Penitentiary," repeated Antonia perfectly, "where Wayne Gale continues his interrupted interview in the middle of a full-scale riot."

A static-filled picture of Wayne appeared on the screens across the country. It was difficult at first to see exactly what was going on, but as the images came in and out of focus, Americans were glued to their seats in shock and wonder at the horrific parade of events.

"This is Wayne Gale reporting live from Batongaville where you can tell by the blood and carnage all around me that the final chapter in the book called Mickey and Mallory has not yet been written," said Wayne, his voice shaking. The camera, swinging wildly on Roger's shoulder, caught the chaos that had erupted throughout the prison. Smoke and gunfire filled the halls. Prisoners were jumping in and out of frame, beating the guards, who were hopelessly outnumbered, and battering each other with frightening ferocity. Wayne was crouching, moving backward as Roger aimed the camera.

"An incredible war has broken out here in Batongaville, unlike anything I've ever seen! Grenada. The Gulf . . . Batongaville . . . will stand alongside them as . . ."

Roger swung the camera wildly to catch Mickey blasting an inmate down the corridor, making way for the train of hostages behind him, which he'd tied with gaffer's tape. Screaming convicts continued to run without direction past the camera, occasionally flitting to a stop to stare or make a face in the camera.

"It was weird, but I actually looked toward Mickey Knox and his gun with a sense of security at that moment," recalls Herb Gaines later. "It was your worst fear come true. Everywhere you looked, people were being hung, raped, impaled. By the time I looked over and saw them hoisting the head of a guard on a pole and carrying it like a totem down the hallway, I knew something had broken loose in this place that I'd only seen in my nightmares."

Kavanaugh's ability to do as he was told by Mickey Knox, namely lead him to Mallory's cell, was made possible by the fact that a group of inmates broke into the main control room, killing three guards in the process, and gaining access not only to all the gates in the prison, which were instantly thrown open, but also to the security files, where—tragically—the names of all the prison informants were kept.

But none of that was on Mickey Knox's mind as he made his way through the corridors toward his date with destiny.

"This is it," said Kavanaugh, pointing with splayed fingers in front of the camera to Mallory's unopened cell door.

In a blinding flash, Mickey kicked through the unlocked door, gun poised. "Honey, I'm home."

What he, and the rest of America was greeted by was an image of Mallory lying crumpled on the floor. In his shoot-first, ask-questions-later mode, Mickey blew Austin away. Lesh was whipping up his gun, firing a round as he was blown across the room by Mickey's shell fire.

Probably before he knew what he was even shooting at, Scagnetti started blasting. His first shots killed *American Maniacs* technician Josh Richmond before he dropped down behind Austin's body for protection. Mickey hit the floor too, poised over the still-warm corpse of Richmond with his shotgun trained on Scagnetti.

Cameras rolling, one of them had to die.

It was like the showdown at the O.K. Corral. On one side Mickey Knox, serial killer extraordinaire, a man with the deadly aim and charisma to captivate a whole nation. On the other Jack Scagnetti, the infamous lawman, defender of the American way, whose crusade for justice made millions of people feel safe about going to sleep at night.

"Looks like we got us a Mexican standoff,"

said Mickey, in words that would etch themselves more firmly in the American consciousness than Arnold Schwarzenegger's "I'll be back" and Rhett Butler's "Frankly my dear, I don't give a damn."

Scott Mabbutt was speechless for the first time in his thirty-two-year broadcasting career. It was the surprisingly plucky Antonia Chavez who struggled for words. "Wayne? Wayne? Can you hear me? What's happening . . . ?"

Antonia's words seem to shake Wayne to life, as the ratings gold this moment represented started to register with him. He took hold of the camera on Roger's shoulder and pointed it directly in Scagnetti's face, oblivious to the fact that if Scagnetti started shooting, Wayne would probably wind up in a heap beside Mickey.

Scagnetti was not backing down. There was too much cop left in him to let this cocksucker get away.

"Slide the shotgun over here, asshole, put your hands behind your head, your forehead on the floor."

"Or what? You'll wound me?" said Mickey, with alarming cool.

"I've never wounded anything in my *life*! I got you locked right between the eyes, Knox."

"If you don't drop that toy, I'm blowin' you in half on three. So, if you got me locked, take the shot. One . . .

Scagnetti didn't flinch.

"Wayne, what's happening?" demanded Chavez.

"Two . . ." said Mickey.

Scagnetti was milliseconds away from squeezing the trigger, when suddenly, and completely unexpectedly, Mickey gave it up.

"All right, Jack, you got me," said Mickey, raising the barrel of his gun in resignation.

Most witnesses to the event at the time, which represented a record-breaking audience of one hundred and twenty million Americans, even by conservative Nielsen estimates, thought that Jack was just so caught up in the giddy victory of the moment that he had completely forgotten about Mallory Knox lying behind him in a mace-inflicted stupor. But in light of revelations that came out later, it was speculated that maybe he was just waiting for Mallory to rise up behind him and finish him off, rather than face the rest of his life on the other side of the law.

Feminist groups weren't so charitable; the more militant among them ascribing Mallory's Phoenix-like rise behind Jack, with a fork in her hand, to divine retribution for what he had done to Haily Robbins. A hundred and twenty million Americans knew what Jack Scagnetti did not at that moment—namely, that his victory was illusory, and his time was up.

With fierce precision, Mallory grabbed Scagnetti brutally by the hair, exposing his throat and jamming an ordinary kitchen fork into it. Scagnetti fell to the floor, choking and helpless.

Wayne was euphoric, watching Mallory stumble over the dead bodies and into Mickey's arms. His innate tabloid-TV instincts kicked in, overcoming even his sense of self-preservation, as he swooped in on the couple with the camera.

"This kiss has been a year in the coming," he said, poking his head in front of them, making sure to expose his good side. "They're doing something everybody told them they would never do again. At this moment they are the only two people on earth."

All America was enraptured, too, as Roger made what was to be his final swan song as a camerman, circling the couple in a 360-degree rotation that dizzied the country, who couldn't believe what was unfolding before their eyes.

For Mickey Knox, it was the fulfillment of the prophecy he'd believed in so firmly that he could journey through hell untouched by fear or doubt.

For Mallory Knox, it was the unbelievable affirmation of her life and love, the undeniable proof that angels did, indeed, watch over her.

For Wayne Gale, it was Neilsen nirvana.

For America, it was the rebirth of romance.

For Jack Scagnetti, it was the end of the road.

Mickey Knox looked down at him, gun in hand. He aimed . . . and fired.

Nothing.

"You lost your touch Jack. You had me. I was out of shells."

There was one last hope, one last chance. With the fork still piercing his throat, Scagnetti was spewing blood and struggling for air as he strained to reach his gun on the floor.

But Mallory Knox was faster. If there was an angel speaking to her as she picked it up and pointed it into his face, it was probably that of Haily "Pinky" Robbins.

"How sexy am I now?" she asked, before sending Scagnetti to meet his maker.

Across America, teenagers everywhere rushed to bars and clubs and town squares to take up candlelight vigils for the Knoxes. Never in the history of the nation had a single incident so united the country's youth in morbid fascination and, horrifically and inexplicably, in support.

They jumped in their cars and took to the roads with wild abandon, in complete disregard for traffic signals or law and order of any sort. The madness that had struck at Batongaville had gone out over the airwaves and radiated throughout the nation. Police gave up trying to apprehend all but the most heinous of offenders, and focused their efforts on trying to contain the mobs. The situation was made worse still by drunken football fans returning home with no idea as to why there seemed to be so many young Dallas fans out that night.

America watched and waited to see if the love of Mickey and Mallory was strong enough yet to deliver them from Batongaville.

CHAPTER
18

The moment Dwight McClusky stepped into the guard post outside the main entrance, he knew he was fucked.

He was on his way out of his office, where he'd just been reamed by the lieutenant governor who was already looking to lay blame for railroading the interview through in the first place, when word reached him of the inmate takeover of the command post inside the main facility. With gates almost everywhere within the prison thrown open, the only thing the inmates couldn't do was get out.

Shawn Devlin was standing behind McClusky as they walked into the guard post, and the full force of what was happening hit him. "Towery was sitting in front of the monitor panel going nuts," recalled Devlin. "I looked up, and it didn't take me but a second to realize why he was flipped out."

Even now, six months later, Devlin's voice

starts to break as the memories flood back. His hand shakes, and he reaches for a reassuring cigarette as he begins to recount the horrors that revealed themselves to him in that moment:

"In the barber shop, I saw Baltin in a barber chair. Two cons were holding him down as another took a straight razor to his throat. Surran was somewhere being held upside down and stuffed into a flaming garbage can. Some poor bastard I didn't even recognize was swinging from one of the rafters in the roundhouse, covered in blood, his neck snapped. And Zoumas . . ." Devlin stops here, struggling for the words to go on. "Zoumas, my fishing buddy, who was in the process of helping me overhaul the motor in my 1968 Camaro 396 R/S . . . well, I don't really want to talk about what they were doing to him in the mess hall. I was almost glad when I'd heard they'd killed him afterwards, 'cause I never wanted to have to look him in the face again after what I'd seen them doing. I knew if it were me, I'd want to be dead."

If Devlin was devastated at the sight of his friends being killed and maimed, McClusky was trembling with rage. It was probably a bad time for Sparky Nimitz, a blues fan from Brooklyn who had moved to Chicago for music two years ago, to deliver the news to the warden:

"They're loose, sir," he said, with trepidation.

At first it didn't register with McClusky what Sparky was talking about. "What?" he said.

"They're . . . they're loose, Boss. Mickey and Mallory Knox are loose."

It started to sink in. "What do you mean, they're loose?"

"They're armed," said Sparky, as it all came spilling out at once. "They got the Wayne Gale crew and Kavanaugh and Homolka. Scagnetti's dead. They got cameras and they're on TV right now!"

McClusky had a frozen look, as if a fuse had blown and his mind had shut down. It took him a moment to recover the power of speech.

"That's it!" he screamed, to no one in particular. "Those two depraved, candy-ass, motherfucking shit-fucks have done this to my prison, and I will see them hang! That's it, Sparky, it's them or me!"

"Sparky was no genius," said Devlin later, "but he knew, like the rest of us, that this was not good news. We'd all heard tell of the Santa Fe prison riots of 1982, everyone called it the 'Devil's Butcher Shop.' Worst prison riot in United States history. But those stories didn't hold a candle to what was happening right before our eyes. And having a guy in charge who was more hell-bent on exacting retribution than he was reestablishing control of the prison—well, it seemed like a great way to get us all killed.

"We were all shocked at his response," said Devlin, "but Sparky was the only one who had the guts to speak up right then."

"What are you talking about, Boss?" said

Sparky. "You got a whole prison going up in flames, and you're diddlin' around with these two pukes."

But McClusky was consumed with rage. "I'll hunt those two rat-bastards down like the pig-fucking junkyard dogs that they are," he sputtered. He gave the order to send in the "green crush," the special tactical unit that was on alert at all times for just such an event, so named because of the fluorescent lime-green jumpsuits they wore.

Devlin was as angry as he was incredulous; he could think of a whole lot better ways to utilize the unit right now, like going in and saving the guards' asses. But he wasn't in charge. McClusky was. And the warden seemed to have only one goal in mind.

"Those two, they die today."

Mickey and Mallory Knox may have been the world's two most famous lovers at that point in time, but they had the innate survival instincts to fight now and love later. What amazed American onlookers was how they seemed to think and move as one unit, communicating in a way that was nonverbal and almost psychic in its intuition about where to go and who was going to come next and from where.

Mickey pulled Wayne aside by his shirt collar. "Hey, good friend, how'd you get here in the first place?"

"My show has a well-appointed news van," said Wayne, all chummy.

"Where's it parked?"

"Out front."

"Well, then that's where we're going. Let me have the keys."

Wayne complied instantly.

"Wagons, hooaa!" cried Mickey.

Somewhere between the cafeteria and the barber shop, Wayne's cellular phone rang. All around him, prisoners were rioting, impervious to the billowing tear gas as they lighted fires and set off homemade grenades. The general sport of killing guards seemed to have given way to torturing snitches, as the supply of live guards was running low and the protective custody ward had been stormed. With the prison's security files in the inmates' hands, there were no secrets anymore. He who had ratted out his fellow inmate was now at his mercy. The demon had taken over.

"Look, honey, nothing happened! I swear! I've been faithful!" Wayne said, as a dying prisoner bumped into him, his scalp sheared clean off and a sign saying SNITCH BITCH on his back. "We'll talk about it when I get home. . . . Of course I'm not okay! This is worse than fucking *Baghdad!* Listen, Dolores, I love you."

He clicked the phone off. "Fucking cow!"

"Come on!" shouted Mickey, as they forced the group down the hall. The hostage train now consisted of Wayne, Julie, Roger, Frank, Kavanaugh, and Homolka. Herb Gaines had taken the opportunity to make a mad dash for an exit door when a prisoner had attacked Wayne in the hallway only moments before, and Mickey was forced to defend him.

"It was pretty clear who Mickey's most valuable hostage was," said Gaines, "and I figured that at that point, his safety depended more on keeping Wayne alive than killing me." Gaines managed to flee the building and hide underneath a pile of garbage that had providentially been left after the lock-down, where he remained until officials were able to secure the prison yard the following day.

Overhead, the lights were flickering on and off when suddenly, from a southern corridor shooting off toward G-Dorm, a troop of green-clad storm troopers came running, guns drawn.

Mickey Knox had no choice but to force his band the other way down the corridor. But waiting for them at the end of this hallway were five armed guards, who had chosen that very place to take a stand.

There seemed no escape.

The guards started firing, and one by one the hostages went down. First Roger, the betacam falling to the ground. Then Julie, as she was desperately pulling at the gaffer's tape around her wrist, trying to extricate herself from Roger's lifeless body. It was no use. Next came Frank, whose chest exploded like a tomato across the hallway.

Wayne Gale freaked. In a split second his brain snapped, and the distinction between good guys and bad guys disappeared in a hail of bullets. In what must have been a mad burst of self-preservation, he ripped free from Kavanaugh and withdrew a Glock semiautomatic from his boot and began firing at the guards as he rolled over the floor and across the hallway for protection.

Mickey and Mallory's luck may have been running out, but they continued to fire anyway, the green crush visible in the distance as the guards at the other end showed no indication of letting up on their fire. Mickey called to Mallory, and without a word she threw him another magazine.

Mickey was reloading when suddenly the shooting stopped. He looked up to see the four guards at the end of the hall. Dead.

It was right then that a man appeared from behind their dead bodies. Skinny, forty, thinning hair—he looked like a civil servant, not a killer.

"Who the fuck are you?" asked Mickey, as he looked at the man with the smoking rifle in his hand that had clearly just laid waste to the five guards.

"I'm Owen," said the man.

"What do you want from us?" asked Mickey.

"I want you to take me with you," said Owen.

It was a helluva place to run into your fan club.

"Right now we're not goin' fuckin' anywhere," said Mickey.

Owen smiled enigmatically. "Follow me," he said.

Whoever this guy was, he was wearing prison blues and he wasn't shooting at them, which was more than Mickey could say for the green storm troopers headed in their direction.

"Come on, baby. Come on, Wayne," he said. "Grab the camera."

"Hello, I'm Antonia Chavez, and if you're just joining us, we're broadcasting live from Batonga-ville Penitentiary, where Wayne Gale is being held hostage by Mickey and Mallory Knox as they make their way through a full-scale prison riot. Wayne, can you hear me?"

Technicians were struggling to bring the image coming through the damaged betacam into focus. Wayne was inside some sort of dark narrow hall-way, and without much light it was difficult to pick out who was still left alive. Wayne was alternately paralyzed with fear as he ducked a spray of gunfire or inexplicably on the phone with his wife, Dolores, whose name soon became the American buzzword for "bitch."

"I don't exactly know where we're going," said Wayne. He had now removed his tie and wrapped it around his head commando-style to cover a gunshot wound to his ear, which was bleeding out of control.

"This is the maintenance corridor between B-

East and West," said Owen in a monotone.
"Those holes you see, they go into every cell.
And all that stuff dripping from the pipes is sew-
age. But it's the best way to get to . . ."

"Shut up," said Mickey. "That thing"—he
pointed to the camera—"is on."

Indeed it was. And outside the prison, Katherine Ginniss was huddled around a Sony Watch-
man with what looked to be a battalion of Illinois
State Police, watching as the drama continued
to unfold.

She had arrived an hour earlier, expecting to
rendezvous with Scagnetti in the warden's office.
Now there was no real reason for her to stay. But
whether it was the macabre fascination that the
rest of the country felt, or simply an indescribable
sense of unfinished business, Katherine Ginniss
watched on as Mickey Knox and his band
emerged from the darkness and slowly made their
way into the light.

They came out of the maintenance corridor on
the second tier of B-East.

Wayne was at the head of the prisoner caravan
of Kavanaugh and Homolka, and waiting for them
was a guard aiming a gun at Wayne.

"Don't shoot—Wayne Gale—don't shoot!"
Wayne screamed. The poor bastard hesitated for
a moment, just in time for Wayne to empty an
entire magazine into him with the Glock.

He blew on the smoking barrel like Dirty

Harry, high on an adrenaline rush that made him feel invincible. Killing had done for him what years of Jungian analysis could not. "I'm alive, for the first time in my life, I'm alive! Thank you, Mickey!"

But Mickey Knox had not gotten stupid since the riot started, and knowing that an idiot with a gun can kill you just as easily from your side as from the other, took the opportunity to disarm Wayne and load him down with the camera.

"You're not centered, man," he told the disappointed journalist.

They turned the corner, ready to descend to the first floor. But at the lower landing, blocking their way to the main corridor and freedom, stood McClusky, flanked by his storm troopers, who had just been successful in retaking the ground floor on B-East.

"End of the line, Knox. Drop 'em!"

Mickey grabbed Kavanaugh and propped him up at the top of the stairwell.

"Don't shoot or I'll kill him, McClusky!" said Mickey.

McClusky noticed what had seemed to escape Mickey in that moment. "He's *dead,* dickweed. You got shit, asshole! Fire!"

Shawn Devlin knew he had crossed over some inexorable line when he and the other storm troopers cut loose and filled Kavanaugh full of bullets, his body dancing wildly as Mickey ducked for cover and grabbed Homolka.

But Mallory was faster, grabbing Wayne

around the neck, pressing her gun against his temple, and propelling herself in front of Mickey on the narrow stairs.

"Back off ya squids or I'll blast him! Back off or I'll blast him!"

None of the deputies lowered their guns. "That guy wasn't someone we really cared about," said Devlin. Wayne started to whimper.

"Don't shoot! I beg you, don't shoot! Please, please, please . . ."

"Shut up Gale, you prick!" cried McClusky, amazed that even in this moment, these two still had the power to cause him grief. "Mickey, Mallory, just let me say—"

"You shut up! I don't wanna hear it," said Mallory.

"I'm sure you realize, Mallory, if you kill this prick, you . . ."

Mallory jerked Wayne backward. "Put up your hand!"

Wayne raised his hand obligingly. Mallory shot a hole in it.

The network censors were so stunned they forgot to bleep Wayne screaming bloody murder.

The deputies jumped back.

Owen appeared from the north side of the stairwell. "Come here, Mickey, I've made a place!"

The camera on Wayne's shoulder swung into the second floor shower on B-East, once gleaming white tile and now covered with blood, looking like a meat market for human flesh. Dead guards and prisoners alike swung from the ceiling, their bodies torn open and entrails hanging out.

The sound of McClusky's voice could be heard yelling up the stairwell.

"Sixty seconds and I'm coming up!"

Who will ever forget the unbearable tension as we all watched what we thought to be Mickey and Mallory Knox's last moments on earth?

Antonia Chavez was now segueing with ease between the panel of hastily arranged experts being fed in from different parts of the country, which included Mickey's Aunt Ophelia, Darryl Gates, a Harvard expert in criminal psychology, and a self-righteously indignant lieutenant governor of the state of Illinois. Antonia managed to fill the dead airtime with commentary and pointed questions. The entire country was watching, depending on her to play tour guide through this orgy of live-action violence.

But no one needed to tell her to interrupt Aunt Ophelia's reminiscences about Mickey's junior prom when it became clear that a showdown was at hand. McClusky had them pinned down, and there was no way he and the angry band of guards that flanked him were going to let them live.

Around the country, the vigils being held for the Knoxes fell silent. Teenage girls began to cry, terrified that the demon lover of their preadolescent dreams was about to be massacred live on network television.

We all watched, breathless with anticipation, as Wayne Gale's cellular phone rang. It was Dolores. But Wayne seemed to finally have found the set of balls the entire nation was hoping he'd locate. In what could be his final moments, he faced his wife with a new sense of empowerment, yelling over the dying cellular battery:

"Blow it off, bitch! You hear me . . . I ain't never comin' home. I'm free of you. I'm *alive!* For the first time I'm *ALIVE.* So guess what— *You piss right off!*"

Wayne hung up on her. And anyone who was holding out any hope that they would all escape felt his heart sink as Mickey bent down to help Mallory bandage a bleeding wound.

"Whatever happens, know I love you . . ." he said, showing the first moment of true tenderness they'd been able to take since their fiery reunion. It seemed important for him to express it at this moment; it might be his last chance. Ever. "I loved you more'n I ever loved myself . . ."

Mallory looked up into his eyes with a sense of love and forgiveness that touched everyone who saw it. "I know. We're not getting out of here, Mickey," she said. "So, I say the hell with going back to our cells. Let's run down these stairs shootin', go out in a hail of bullets, an' take as many of these motherfuckers with us as we can."

Mickey saw the future she was looking into. But it was a future he was unwilling to accept for the woman he loved.

"That's poetry," he said. "But we'll do that when all else fails."

His exhaustion suddenly lifting, a plan seemed to take shape in his mind. He stood, confronting the hysterical Duncan Homolka.

"You married?"

"I don't wanna die!" whimpered Homolka.

Mickey slapped him into his senses. "I said, are you married?"

Meanwhile, Wayne was on the cellular phone once again, this time announcing his newfound emancipation to his girlfriend, Ming. "I'm gonna come over tonight with a tab of ecstasy and put a hot pepper up your . . ."

Ming didn't seem to be as taken with the new Wayne as Wayne was, as signaled by the click he heard on the other end of the line.

"Ming? Ming!" cried Wayne, finally dashing the cellular phone against the wall, much to the relief of everyone watching, who had long since tired of hearing about Wayne's domestic problems.

"Respected journalist!" called Mickey, who was in the process of taping the barrel of his rifle to Duncan Homolka's neck. "Wayne, I'd like you to meet Duncan Homolka," he said, as he began doing likewise to Wayne, who said "hello" to Duncan as Mickey twisted gaffer's tape around his neck.

"The only way we're gonna get all the way to the front door is if they don't want to kill you more than they want to kill us,'' said Mickey. "On your knees, Wayne.''

Mickey grabbed the video camera and lifted it to his shoulder.

"You wanted reality, Wayne?''

"My name is Wayne Gale! I am the star of *American Maniacs!*''

Wayne came into view of McClusky and the guards, camera in his hands—filming himself.

"I looked up and saw Mickey's right hand taped to the trigger and stock of a shotgun that was wrapped firmly to Wayne's neck,'' said Devlin.

"Watched by forty million people every week!'' continued Wayne in a voice filled with hysteria. "I am a respected journalist, winner of the Edward R. Murrow Award among many others!''

McClusky froze, not knowing what to do, wanting nothing so much as to throttle Mickey with his bare hands, which he would probably have done had Sparky Nimitz not held him back.

"We realized right then that if we took out either Mickey or Mallory, either Wayne or Homolka would die. We might've taken the chance if there hadn't been a camera there, but the idea of becoming one of the cops in the Rodney King case—put on trial by people who just watched a video tape and weren't there and couldn't know how you felt—well, none of us wanted to do that,'' Devlin said later.

Which was what Mickey Knox was counting on.

"You are on camera," cried Wayne. *"We are live.* If anybody puts me in danger, my network will sue Dwight McClusky and the entire sheriff's department and the governor himself. My estate will sue every officer personally who fires . . ."

Mickey knew what he was doing. It had an effect on the deputies.

"Make a path!" yelled Mallory, and the wall of deputies started moving back.

The camera tracked the caravan as, miraculously they made their way, moving as if under one tent. Across from them a phalanx of guns and lawmen, moving in unison, made a parallel track out of the stairwell and into the final corridor approaching the reception area to the prison.

Freedom. On the other side of the gates.

Wayne was yelling, Duncan blubbering. The deputies kept their guns trained, but they gave ground—parting like the Red Sea.

But as the gates came into sight, McClusky positioned himself in front of them.

"How far do you think you're going to get?"

"Right out the front door," said Mickey with eerie confidence.

"That'll never happen," said McClusky.

But it was happening. The caravan marched forward, Wayne and Duncan shouting their mantras. Nobody dared move on them.

"We were completely frustrated and humiliated," said Devlin.

Mickey and McClusky were nose to nose as the caravan edged forward.

"I will personally hunt you down, blow the head off your fucking-whore wife, and plant your sick ass in the ground all by myself," said McClusky.

But Mickey's cool was unshakeable. "Another day, but not today, Warden."

McClusky looked like he was going to pop his cerebral cortex. Which, indeed, he did. Medical experts later determined from close examination of the videotape that this is probably when Dwight McClusky's heart attack began.

"The guard on the other side of the gate, Pruce, saw us all edging down the hallway, and he saw the camera, too. He didn't want to be the one to precipitate a showdown. If McClusky had turned to him and told him not to open the doors, he probably wouldn't have. But McClusky was starting to buck with pain just then, so Pruce opened up, and Mickey and Mallory went right on through."

Mickey closed the doors behind them. The camera went with Mickey and Mallory down the stairs and outside the prison to freedom. Trees. Birds. No bars.

What the camera didn't record was the hundreds of angry prisoners who had broken their way through the guards' blockade and were now running toward McClusky with shotguns, sticks, numchuks, razors, and broken chairs.

"Before he left and closed the door, Mickey

had waved Pruce into the corridor, so there was no way for us to get out. We started shooting into the mob, and dozens fell, but there were more behind them. They just kept on coming,'' Devlin remembered.

McClusky climbed the bars, grabbing at the only protection he had, his mace, and spraying it on the blood-frenzied crowd in a pathetic attempt to save his own life. They tore him down from the bars, his heart seizing up as they passed him over their heads from hand to hand like a stage diver at a rock concert.

"The last thing I saw before I went down was McClusky's head being hoisted on a stick and passed through the crowd," recalled Devlin, who was left for dead beneath the bodies of his fallen comrades.

CHAPTER
19

Against all conventional logic, Mickey and Mallory Knox had simply walked out of the highest security prison in America, with nothing more than shotguns taped underneath the chins of their hostages.

With the camera rolling, none of the state police, National Guard or Highway Patrol officers who were standing watch outside the prison dared defy Mickey Knox's orders not to send any official-looking vehicles after the *American Maniacs* news van.

Which left only unmarked cars available to follow Mickey and Mallory as they escaped through the Joliet countryside.

One of those vehicles was the rental car belonging to Katherine Ginniss.

Amidst the post-Superbowl traffic and the general mayhem on the roads caused by marauding teenagers who were hot-rodding in support of

Mickey and Mallory's escape, the van managed to evade almost everyone who was following it. Those who managed to get through, gave chase until Mickey suddenly turned onto a rural road, and Mallory threw Duncan Homolka out the back of the van. The resulting squeal of brakes and tire smoke left a four-car pileup as unmarked cars tried to dodge the rolling body.

Yet as fate would have it, there was one remaining roadblock.

Katherine Ginniss had chosen County Road 5, going south, on what appeared to be little more than a lucky hunch. Mickey Knox had picked the same road, going north. They passed each other at seventy-five miles an hour, forcing Ginniss to slow almost to a stop before turning to head after them. It was a basic U-turn, no fancy tire squealing. If four years of D.C. traffic had taught her anything, it was that less was more.

She raced the Ford Taurus over ninety miles an hour, the highest number printed on the speedometer. If she tried to use her cellular phone to radio in the Knoxes position, as she almost certainly would, she couldn't get a line, the airwaves being packed with police chatter.

She must've known that there was no means of stopping the van—having no weapon at all, while Mickey and Mallory were by all accounts armed to the teeth. The safest plan would be to drop back and follow at a distance, eventually finding a line and contacting the police to set up roadblocks. Common sense, standard operating procedure.

But Katherine Ginniss had spent far too long behind an FBI desk, letting others take the glory while she sifted through the reams and reams of paperwork that made their jobs possible.

She gunned the engine beyond the red line.

The Taurus charged into the van's rear bumper with an impact that crumpled the rental car's grille and smashed in both of her headlights.

Inside the van, the jolt took everyone by surprise. Mallory loaded both barrels of the shotgun, and prepared to take down this last threat.

"Why don't they give it up, baby?" shouted Mallory over the engine's roar.

It was Wayne who answered. "The wolf doesn't know why he's a wolf, and the deer doesn't know why he's a deer. God just made it that way, right, Mickey?" he said, in a statement that would later lead psychologists to speculate that Wayne Gale was now suffering from Patty Hearst syndrome, the overwhelming fear of the situation having driven him into sympathy with his captors.

Others would conclude he was just an idiot.

Mickey smiled and swerved, trying to knock the Taurus off the road. "Comin' at you from the left, Mal!" he shouted.

As Mallory prepared to fire, Owen Traft was watching out the back windows of the van, his face pressed against the glass. Time slowed as he watched Ginniss behind the wheel of the car, determined to take down the van or die.

His gaze never leaving the Taurus, he began to pull off his shoes and socks and unbutton his shirt.

"What the fuck are you doing?" shouted Wayne, watching the man get naked in the back of the van.

"Nah, let him do it," Mallory replied. "It's like he's got some kind of mission. Maybe he's some kind of angel, sent to help us. Deliver us from evil."

Angel or not, Owen Traft was now naked, crouched in the back of the van. Wayne watched in a blur as Owen opened the back door to a rush of air that swirled papers in the van. Mickey wasn't letting up on the accelerator for a second.

Ginniss had dropped back about thirty feet, anticipating a hail of bullets.

What she saw instead was a naked man crouched like a golem in the back of the van, his eyes staring straight at her car. And before she could react, he was leaping straight at her.

In midair, Owen Traft tucked into the fetal position, a cannonball dive perfected during childhood summers at the city pool. The base of his spine was the first thing to hit, the impact shattering the windshield in a thousand spiderweb cracks that gave way as his entire body broke through. Ginniss died as the force snapped three vertebrae in her neck, the airbag firing later as the Taurus careened off the road and into a drainage ditch.

Mallory Knox climbed up in the passenger seat by her husband. "Did you see that, Mickey? He flew. I swear to God, he was flying. Can you even believe that shit?"

"It's all a mystery, baby," he said, cradling her chin in his hand. "Who's to say? I mean really, who's to say?"

As he started his standup for the final interview of his career, Wayne Gale seemed reasonably calm and collected, positioned against the verdant foliage of the rural Illinois landscape. Despite his many cuts and abrasions, plus the bullet hole through his hand, he pulled off a fairly convincing war-correspondent bravado. He was no Scud Stud like Arthur Kent, but Wolf Blitzer would have been proud.

The scene that finally reached American homes was occasionally out of synch, due to damage sustained by the betacam during the riot, but there was no doubt as to what was happening.

"This is Wayne Gale—unfortunately we're all no longer 'alive.' I'm wounded and my crew is dead."

Mallory Knox was behind the camera, toying with the zoom and focus buttons, in a playful mood now that the police were no longer on their tail.

"I have left my wife, and my girlfriend has left me," continued Wayne, taking a moment to revel in his own personal melodrama. "Mickey Knox's plan worked. We walked out the front door, into the news van, and made our getaway. When we were followed by patrol cars, Mallory Knox killed Deputy Sherrif Duncan Homolka and tossed his body out the back."

Mallory had actually thrown Homolka out of the van still very much alive, and in fact he survived, but Wayne's version made for better copy.

"Mickey told authorities over my police band that I would surely be next if they didn't give up pursuit. Why helicopters weren't deployed, I don't know. My only thought is that it happened too fast for arrangements to be made. We've just pulled off the road to do this interview. Tensions run high—"

"We ain't got all fuckin' day!" shouted Mickey from off screen.

Wayne moved to take the camera from Mallory's shoulder and turn it around on the couple. "Without any further ado, Mickey and Mallory. . . ."

Mallory took a minute to adjust her prison clothing and preen before the camera as Wayne began the interview. "Mallory Knox, what were you thinking about during this extraordinary escape!" said Wayne, who was now beginning to recover, and clearly sensed that the opportunity he had before him could well be the greatest journalistic coup of his career.

"I wondered how long it would be before we'd

get to be alone together," said Mallory. "And I wondered if I could wait that long."

Mickey and Mallory began to snuggle like two lovebirds in anticipation of their romantic reunion. But Wayne Gale wanted a few answers first.

"Did you have anything to do with the riot?"

"We had nothing to do with that riot. That riot was just—whatchamacallit—"

"Fate," volunteered Mickey.

"Fate," said Mallory. "We just didn't know jack shit about any riot. How are we supposed to organize a riot when we've been in fuckin' isolation for the past year, Wayne? I mean, it's not like we care . . . If they wanna say we masterminded the whole thing, let 'em. It won't exactly keep us up at night or anything. But the truth is"—Mallory smiled at her lover, with the confidence of a woman whose faith in the universe has just been reaffirmed—"it was fate."

"And fate it was!" said Wayne. "And this is *American Maniacs*—"

Mickey snapped his fingers. "C'mon, c'mon, let's hurry this up."

But Wayne clearly felt safe with the two now, and he was reverting to his old, pushy self. "One more question, one more question. So, what's next?"

Mallory embraced Mickey. "Well, now me and Mickey are gonna take it easy. Maybe lie in a big kingsize bed for a couple of days. Just enjoy each other's company. And I been thinkin' about motherhood. I think me and Mickey are gonna get started on that real soon.''

Mallory giggled knowingly as she put her head onto Mickey's shoulder. He rubbed her head fondly. But the realization that time was running short, and two killers on the run couldn't stay in one place for very long was beginning to weigh on Mickey Knox, who still had one more thing to do.

"Gotta go . . ." he said.

"Wait!" cried Wayne, unwilling to let this virtual career-annuity plan disappear. "How do you two intend to disappear? You're probably the most famous couple in America."

"Well, back in slave times they had a thing called the underground railroad . . ."

"Okay, end of interview," said Mickey, wary that Mallory would go on to reveal plans that could jeopardize their hard-won freedom.

The camera went haywire as Wayne lowered it. "Okay, just let me swing around and film myself asking the questions. Then I'll do my little wrap-up and we're off."

No one who was watching was prepared for what came next.

"Oh, we're gonna do a little wrap-up all right, Wayne. But it won't be you starin' in the camera, lookin' dumb and actin' stupid," said Mickey, as he picked up his shotgun. "Instead, you're gonna be starin' down the barrels of our shotguns and we're gonna be pullin' the triggers."

Wayne forced a disbelieving chuckle. "This is a joke, right?"

Mickey pumped his shotgun in response.

"Just wait one fucking minute," said Wayne. "Wait! I kinda felt that during this . . . this whole escape thing that a kind of bond developed between the three of us. We're kinda in this together, right?"

"No, not really," said Mickey. "You're scum, Wayne. You did it for the ratings. You didn't give a shit about us or about anything, Wayne, except yourself. That's why nobody really gives a shit about you. That's why 'helicopters were not deployed.' "

A look of mounting horror came over Wayne's face. "Wait! What about the Indian?"

"What about him?" said Mickey.

"Didn't you say you were finished with killing? Didn't you say 'love beats the demon?' "

"I am, and it will," said Mickey, who was clearly beginning to be annoyed with Wayne at this point. "It's just that you're the *last one,* Wayne."

Wayne broke down and started to cry. "No, man, don't fucking kill me."

He seemed to have touched a tender spot in Mickey's heart, for Mickey came over and put a hand on his shoulder. "It's not about you, you egomaniac. I sort of like you. It's just that killing you, and what you represent is a sort of . . . statement," said Mickey. More privately, into Wayne's ear, Mickey whispered: "I'm not exactly one hundred percent sure what it's saying, but . . ."

Wayne must have thought that in this moment of intimacy, Mickey might be softening. He turned and ran, scampering vainly through the woods.

Mickey called after him. "Wayne!" he cried. "Wayne!"

The journalist stopped, crumpling in defeat.

"Have some dignity," said Mickey.

If Wayne was going to check out, he wasn't going without having the last word.

"All right, all right, so I'm a parasite," he said, resigning himself to his fate as he walked back to the armed duo. "It's a cruel world out there. You were wronged. So what else is new? The day you killed, your ass belonged to us. You did what you had to do. So did I. We're married."

Mallory Knox started laughing—whether at Wayne's new level of self-awareness or the thought of blasting him into eternity is not known.

The wheels in Wayne's shrewd little brain had not stopped turning, however. He decided to give it one last attempt. "Think about it. The point is we can do a Salman Rushdie thing next—books, talk shows, all remote. We move around, duckin' and bobbin', then we come up for air once in a while. *Donahue, Oprah,* do you know how big we could be?"

Whatever Wayne Gale was selling, Mickey

Knox wasn't buying it. "Let's make a little music, Colorado," he said.

"Wait! Wait!" cried Wayne. "Don't Mickey and Mallory always leave somebody alive to tell the tale?"

"We are," they said in tandem. "Your camera."

Wayne Montclaire Galenovitch stretched his arms out to embrace the universe, letting out a cry of "Om" as the Knoxes pumped seventeen shells into him.

The American public was stunned as they watched Wayne's body slump into the tree behind him. With birds singing, the leaves of the tree fluttering in the wind, the last thing the camera recorded before the network cut the feed was Mickey Knox putting his arm around his bride and walking off into the sunset.

"Wayne? Wayne?" cried Antonia Chavez, whose valiant effort to maintain composure during the entire incident was finally shattered. "Oh, my God."

Scott Mabbutt was unwilling to watch her fall apart on national TV after having held up so well during the whole affair. Without asking anyone's permission, he switched over to a prerecorded tape of the six o'clock news, a decision that would later cost him his job. Ironically, the anchor was reporting on a massacre at a wedding reception the night before.

He went down to the floor to put his arm

around Antonia and give her a silent congratulations on a job well done. He'd never taken her seriously as a journalist before, never considered her anything but a talking head with nice hair and a good set of teeth. She collapsed onto his shoulder, sobbing quietly for a few seconds as the emotional drain of the event started to take its toll, before rousing some heretofore unseen inner strength and pulling herself together.

"How come nobody ever discovered you were such a tough cookie before?" asked Mabbutt.

She looked at him as if the answer was obvious.

"Nobody ever asked."

CHAPTER
20

Dear Nora,

You probably don't remember me, but we met at the Las Vegas convention you sponsored on "angels." You probably didn't know who I was at the time, but since then you've probably heard about me if you own a TV.

I just wanted to write and let you know how much I was affected by the conference, and tell you that you changed my life. I don't want you to get in trouble or anything for getting this letter, so if you're worried about whether you can show it to the police or not, well go right ahead 'cause I sent it to a friend who sent it to a friend who sent it to a friend (Mickey's idea) and so there's no way they can trace the postmark. He's pretty clever like that, Mickey is, I think he's got a gift for evading police detection.

Anyway, since I don't really have any family or friends left from when I was growing up (you'd be surprised how people react when they find out you killed your parents) I wanted to let someone know what had happened to us after our escape and say that we were doing well.

I hope you publish this in your newsletter and let folks know that if people think we were lucky, I ascribe our luck to angels. I have one on my shoulder. She sits there every day and boy is her job tough. She's gotta keep a constant eye on Mickey and his demons, because if you turn your back for a minute the next thing you know boom they're outa control.

After we shot that journalist fellow, Mickey promised me that it would be our last killing. I was still pretty pissed off at him for killing the Indian and all, but I was so glad to see him again after a year that it didn't seem like a good time to make an issue of it. I never knew a body could love someone so much that fate would just have to reunite them, no matter what obstacles stood in the way. But when I saw Mickey come into my cell with that shotgun, I knew that there was nothing that could keep us apart, not even death, which is why I wasn't scared to die with him if that's what it took.

Fortunately, it didn't come to that, and we set off with Mickey vowing to turn over a new leaf. No more killing, we were going straight. But it couldn't've been more than an hour before that promise was tested.

The van we were in was running out of gas, and we had to pull into a gas station to refill. It was a Shell station, I think. We took the trouble to scrounge around the van for some spare change, 'cause we didn't have any money, just so we could pay for the gas and not have to kill anyone in the process.

So Mickey walks up to the man in the little booth

and puts down the money. But the guy was on the phone with his girlfriend or something I think. Mickey just stands there, looking over at me in the van, and I know what he's thinking, normally I would kill this guy but see how good I'm being, I ain't even got my gun drawn, aren't you proud of me? And I smiled, because I was. Thinking about how handsome he was, and how he was struggling to be a good person and all.

But this asshole was determined to test Mickey or something, I don't know, because he just kept talking and talking and wouldn't pay any attention to Mickey. And I could see Mickey was starting to get hot under the collar. So he knocks on the glass.

"S'cuse me, amigo, but I'm in sort of a hurry," Mickey says. The guy just keeps talking, so Mickey bangs on the glass, harder this time. The guy finally turns and says to Mickey that can't he see he's busy. Mickey says well isn't his job supposed to be to take people's money so they can pump gas. The guy just ignores him.

Mickey came running back to the van for his shotgun. I guess if you've got an established way of dealing with problems, and it's been very successful in the past, it's hard to break your old habits. And to tell the truth, the little peckerwood pissed me off, too. I sure don't like to hear anybody talk like that to my baby.

But I knew if we killed this one we'd just go on killing and killing and killing, and my angel said to me "Mallory, it's time you and Mickey took another road."

So I put my hand on his arm, and I didn't need to even say nothing, because me and Mickey we know what each other's going to think before we even say it. He looked into my eyes, and I saw that demon flash inside him for a second, but I guess he and saw my angel too, and put down the shotgun.

So he punched the guy senseless and we went to another gas station.

As we pulled away from the pump, I yelled after him, "This is the luckiest day of your entire life, fucker!"

Now I will tell you about the pride and joy of my life, my baby Farrah.

She is an angel on earth. She's got blonde hair like Mickey and plenty of it. Mickey and me, we never knew that someone else could be so beautiful and so perfect as Farrah. I was a little bit worried before she first came into our lives, that Mickey would even love her more than me. But I'm so stuck on her now, everything I think and do has Farrah in the middle of it. I swear, Nora, she is an angel born on earth.

You should see her and Mickey play together. It's the perfect picture of a happy family. I don't know how such a thing happened, after all we been through, but here we are. (I can't tell you exactly where that is, but you'll have to trust me, it's great.) You'd think, as famous as we were there for a while, that we couldn't go anywhere without being recognized and that some-body would turn us in. But them media people, they're always latching onto something new, and it's been over a year now. Sometimes I even get a little sad, I feel like we've been replaced. But I guess it's worth being forgotten if it means we can be together to raise Farrah.

The only problem we still got, and it's one we have to work on every day, is Mickey's eye for the ladies. Which never ceases to chap my ass. After all we've been through, you think he'd have some respect for me and my feelings. Which he does, to the extent that he understands them, which isn't much. But he's smart enough to know that he could wake up one morning with his balls stuffed in his mouth, and that I'm just the girl to do it, so he manages to keep his pants zipped. Ain't it ironic how sometimes in life, you wind up with just what you deserve?

I could go on and on, but there isn't really that much more to tell that's interesting. Since we stopped killing people, our lives just aren't as dramatic as they used to be. It's all small things, like changing diapers and playing with babies and being with our friends. Which we have a surprising amount of, considering. They've been really helpful in establishing our new life, and we're really thankful. It was great when that movie producer found us and paid us all that money for our life stories so that we could stop living off their generosity, but I guess I shouldn't say anything more about that, Mickey he gets mad and calls me a big mouth.

Again, I want to thank you for all you done for me and the work you do on behalf of angels. I think you're an angel yourself, Nora. And you can tell people not to worry about me and Mickey.

We're doing just fine.

Love,
Mallory Knox

Postscript

Reuters—Newhall, CA—Police today arrested fifteen-year-old Sara Wu and her sixteen-year-old boyfriend, Garret Reynolds, in connection with the murder of her parents, Frederick and Mai-Ling Wu, the Newhall couple who were shot to death in their beds last Friday evening.

The two were arrested after a highschool friend, whom police refuse to identify, came forward and admitted that the two had been overheard bragging about the killing at the local Ben & Jerry's ice cream shop where they'd gone for dessert after the murder.

Although there was no apparent motive for the killing, police spokesmen acknowledge that gunpowder stains on a long blond wig and suede hotpants found in Sarah's closet indicate that the murder may be another in the Mickey and Mallory Knox copycat killings that experts now estimate to be between 120 and 150 in number.

The families of the two teenagers refused comment, except to announce that attorney Justin P. Stanley of Beverly Hills was representing both parties in negotiations with the four television networks for rights to the story.

Epilogue

MICKEY and MALLORY KNOX are currently still at large, although the FBI investigation as to their whereabouts continues. Their official fan club, the Owen Traft Society, has a membership of over 15,000, who each pay $35 a year for a newsletter and memorabilia relating to the two.

NORA HAFFERTY's cable TV show, *Angel Talk,* is one of the top five-rated shows on her network. She is also working on a book to be published by Penguin Books this spring.

ANTONIA CHAVEZ went on to sign a three-year, eight-million-dollar contract with NBC who won her services in a bidding war involving all three major networks. The third-place network hopes to install her in her own prime-time show next season in its latest attempt to compete with ABC's successful *20/20* and CBS's juggernaut *60 Minutes*. It will ironically run in the time slot formerly occupied by Wayne Gale's *American Maniacs*.

SIMON and NORMAN HUN's attempts to franchise their gym MUSCLE 2000 failed and the two filed Chapter 11 bankruptcy last year.

SHAWN DEVLIN resigned his position as a guard at Batongaville Penitentiary following the Knox riots. His movie-star good looks, however, were spotted by casting directors as his face appeared alongside Dwight McClusky's in the B-Wing standoff during the riots, and he subsequently signed a two-picture deal with producer Mosha Diamant to appear in action films. His first movie, *Bulletproof,* in which he appears as Dolf Lundgren's sidekick, will be released in May.

DUNCAN HOMOLKA survived his ordeal of being thrown out of the back of the *American Maniacs* van during the escape. After his recovery, he was paid $100,000 for an exclusive interview with a tabloid TV show, and began a speaking tour on his experiences with Mickey and Mallory Knox. He currently commands up to $25,000 per appearance.

RANDALL KREVNITZ is currently a junior at the University of Illinois. He drives a 1970 Dodge Challenger 383 Magnum RT convertible and refuses to ride in Fords.

DON MURPHY is currently under FBI investigation for being the only man on earth persistent enough to have successfully contacted Mickey and Mallory Knox following their escape, securing the rights to their life stories. Along with his partner, Jane Hamsher, he is currently producing a feature film for New Regency Entertainment/ Warner Brother Pictures based on the Knoxes, to be directed by Oliver Stone.

SPARKY NIMITZ moved back to Brooklyn, became a sidekick on Howard Stern's morning show and opened his own blues club.

WANDA BISBING resigned from the district attorney's office, changed her name, and has never been heard from again.